LITTLE MUTILATIONS

THREE BODY HORROR NOVELLAS

JESS LANDRY, SOFIA AJRAM, AND NADIA BULKIN

BOOK 7 IN CRYSTAL LAKE'S DARK TIDE SERIES

Let the world know:
#IGotMyCLPBook!

Crystal Lake Publishing
www.CrystalLakePub.com

WELCOME
TO ANOTHER

CRYSTAL LAKE PUBLISHING
CREATION

Subscribe to Crystal Lake Publishing's Dark Tide series for updates, specials, behind-the-scenes content, and a special selection of bonus stories - http://eepurl.com/hKVGkr

THE NIGHT BELONGS TO US

JESS LANDRY

1

MARY DANGLED THE necklace in between her fingers, letting the closed locket spin. It reminded her of when her daughter, Laura, was young, how they would dance and twirl and fall onto the patchy brown carpet in their shitty rundown apartment, the one that Mary paid an arm and a leg for in rent.

Simpler times, she thought, when they would laugh about nothing, Laura's giggles enough to break even the coldest of spirits; when they knew what each other was thinking; when they would disappear together into make-believe worlds of Laura's doing—anything to escape their reality, a reality that grew bleaker every passing day with Mary unable to work and her government payments barely putting food on their second-hand table.

The light coming in through the only window in the room hit the gold at just the right spot, casting a glint in her eye as the locket continued to twirl. Inside, a picture of Laura, maybe five, maybe seven, of that Mary wasn't sure. Laura had found the gold necklace on the street and given it to Mary as a gift, placing the only photo Laura could find of herself inside. Mary had sworn to Laura that she'd never take the necklace off, that she'd wear it around her neck, hanging at her heart, for always.

But that promise had been made a long time ago, when Laura was little and still believed the white lies that Mary often told.

Mary tucked a strand of her long, raven-black hair behind her ear and looked to the window, the glass shattered from neglect and time. Snow drifted behind the broken pane, the occasional flake finding its way into the room, softly fluttering down the peeling wallpaper and rotted wainscoting, the only memories of what this space once was. She'd assumed it had been an office, given its size—the office of someone important, until they'd abandoned this building like all the others in the area. Mary watched a single flake twirl onto the grated floor, only to disappear at the first touch, absorbed into the metal like it had never existed.

The metal grated flooring, as far as she knew, was a recent addition.

She'd spent the past few days in this room along with three others, all spread out across the uncomfortable floor. Days without a proper meal. Days without a hot shower or clean clothes or contact with the outside world. Just a broken window to remind her what was out there. A reminder of everything she wanted to leave behind.

She'd come to learn some of the rooms' little secrets—the sloped secondary floor underneath the metal one, the one that caved in the centre, leading into a drain that travelled deep into the depths of the building; the muffled voices, sometimes sounding like screams, that rose from the drain pipe, finding their way into her ears while she tried to sleep; and the impenetrable rusted steel door, the one that led to a safe place, a quiet place, somewhere she could live out the rest of her days without having to worry about food or shelter . . . or Laura.

It was the whole reason she was there, after all. The whole reason any of them were.

Beyond the rusted door was where they needed to go.

It was where they belonged.

From behind a less important door—a weak wooden one that led back to humanity—footsteps echoed, growing closer and closer with every passing second.

The others in the room, women like Mary, cast out from society, shunned by their families, women looking for something more, something better—despite knowing the steep cost—all sat up, ready for their awaited visitor. A visitor with either a gift or a curse. Mary was never quite sure which to expect.

The other door slowly creaked open, and in stepped Cee. The low light from one working sconce cast strange, sharp shadows on her soft but angular face, a face riddled with scars that somehow only made her more intriguing. The light made her short, dark hair seem even darker. It made her wide eyes simmer like two black coals after a long burn, the flames still alive and well inside her.

Mary let her locket go back to its resting spot over her heart as she and the three other women stood, keeping their heads low and their eyes down.

Cee's heavy boots clanged against the metal floor, slowly, methodically, as she passed by each of the women, sizing them up, seeing if they were fit for the next step of initiation.

There'd been six of them on day one. Six women in a cold room, waiting to see if they'd be invited past the metal door.

One went the first day. Another a few days later.

They'd both failed their initiations, unable to stomach what Cee had asked of them, unable to see the bigger picture, which was as clear to Mary as the snow falling outside—survival.

The first two hadn't wanted it enough.

But Mary did.

And failure wasn't an option.

"You." Cee's voice was like her features, soft yet sharp. Mary kept her eyes down, her gaze focused on the drain beneath the floor, shadows of the other nights' stains still haunting her. "It's your turn."

Mary raised her head slowly, still not meeting Cee's eyes, instead directing her gaze to Cee's shoulders, small but bulky, no thanks to the layers of old clothing she wore.

"Are you ready?"

Mary nodded.

Cee said no more. She moved back toward the wood door while the other women in the room moved to one side, as close together as they could.

Mary glanced up. All their eyes were on her. They were waiting to see if she had it in her. They were waiting for her to fail.

Cee stepped out into the darkened hallway beyond the room, her boots shuffling against the debris of the abandoned building, echoing out into the nothingness.

Then, a man entered, stumbling into the small space with drunken laughter.

He wiped spittle from his open mouth, his eyes slowly focusing on the room around him, all comprehension lost.

"What's all this?" he muttered.

Cee stepped back into the room, closing the wood door, and placed a hand on the man's shoulder. Mary, for the briefest of moments, looked at Cee, studying as much of her face as she could.

The softness had disappeared.

There was something terrifying in her androgynous features that Mary couldn't turn away from.

Something primal.

"Hey," the man said, attempting to shake Cee's grip and spin toward her, but her strength was much more than what it seemed.

Cee forced him to the centre of the room, pushing him down to his knees, facing the metal door, without so much as a grunt. He knelt directly over the drain.

Mary took her place between the man and the metal door, a nervous energy creeping into her body.

She had to do this.

The man's gaze scattered about the room, shooting from one woman to another, as the realization of the situation hit him. "Let me go," he pleaded. "Stop."

But none moved.

Cee pulled a rusted blade from her back pocket, passing it to Mary.

Mary took it with a shaking hand, failing to steady herself before Cee caught wind. She wanted Cee to believe she was confident, that she had what it took to be welcomed past the door. She let the blade rest in her palm, trying to focus her mind on its cool touch. It had seemed so heavy in the hands of the others, as though Cee had passed them a boulder, but there, in Mary's, it was as light as a feather. Still, the tremble would not leave. She tried to will it away, but it wouldn't stop—her body knew exactly what she was trying to force herself to do.

"Please . . . I have a family . . . "

The others that had come through the door in short time there had said the same thing. Mary had wondered if that were true, or if that was just something people said when they knew they were about to die.

"Go on," Cee snapped, waking Mary from her thoughts.

Mary took the first step toward the man, her own footsteps as loud as a crack of thunder. The man thrashed and pulled and screamed, but Cee's grip kept him pinned down.

Closer. Blade out.

Is it worth it?

Closer. Tighten grip.

Do I really want it that bad?

Closer. Smell his fear.

What would Laura think?

Mary brought the dull blade to the man's rough skin.

Do it, she coaxed herself.

She tried to drag the blood-encrusted edge along his neck, but something was preventing her hand from obeying.

Do it!

She tried again, willing her hand to move. It didn't budge.

Do it or die!

Going against the very will of her own body, Mary jerked her hand forward.

The movement was quick. Sloppy.

And the result was not what she wanted.

The dull blade had scraped at the man's skin, the smallest nick slowly filling with a hint of red. A tiny drop of blood seeped through, barely enough for a Band-Aid.

The blade hit the grated metal floor at the same time as Mary's knees. Mary screamed into the metal, into the drain, like a signal to the voices down below, those screaming up at her, those living where she wanted to be.

A dream that would never happen now.

She was just like the others.

A failure.

The man seemed to relax, a glimmer of hope shuddering through his body.

"Jesus," Cee muttered from above, unimpressed by yet another disappointment.

Mary peeled herself up off the floor, wet stinging eyes looking up at Cee, the fear of meeting her gaze now long dissolved.

Mary watched in awe as Cee raised her free hand above the man's head, keeping him still and in place.

Then, Cee brought her hand across the man's neck with a movement so refined it was like a conductor commanding her orchestra.

A splash of warmth struck Mary's face, little dabs of heat on her cheek, near her eyes, on her mouth. On impulse, she licked her lips, lapping up the liquid, the taste of metal striking her tongue almost immediately, almost satisfying.

Mary's gaze turned to the man.

His eyes went wide as his hands fumbled to his throat. But it was too late—the jagged gash in his skin tore open and his blood began to spill.

The man gargled, the blood filling his lungs, then finding its path out of his body and trickling onto his clothes.

And down it all went, out of him and into the drain below.

The others behind Mary watched. Another letdown, she imagined them thinking. A better chance for them to make it past the door when their time came.

Mary's gaze fell to Cee's hand, the nail on her index finger sharper than a shard of glass. Cee brought her finger in front of her, studying the small chunks of gore that had gotten stuck under her nail, then put her finger into her mouth, sucking at what little was there. She took a deep breath, the tease of blood satiating whatever hunger she may have had. Mary watched on with a jealous eye—she wanted that hunger, that desire. She wanted what Cee had.

Cee continued to grip the man's shoulder with her other hand, then, without any effort at all, released him. His lifeless body clunked onto the grated floor, his blood flowing even more freely into the drain.

The blood sucked clean from her finger, Cee now turned her attention to Mary.

"Please . . . " Mary sat on her knees, now the one who pleaded, unable to contain her tears any longer. "I need to be here. I belong here."

"Doesn't look that way," Cee said, emotionless.

Mary locked her bloodied hands in front of her, almost in prayer, with the necklace chain and her raven-dark hair interwoven between her fingers like a morbid rosary.

"I can give you something else. Anything you want. Anything at all."

Cee looked down at Mary. The light coming in through the only window in the room hit Mary's necklace at just the right spot, casting a golden glint in Cee's dark eyes.

II

The Greyhound bus pulled into the snowed-covered depot, a depot as lifeless and cold as its final destination: Winnipeg, directly in the heart of Canada.

The bus driver cranked the door open, letting the few weary travellers debark from the slow, icy ride they'd been subjected to for the past several hours. Out they filed, exhausted, just as lifeless and cold as their surroundings.

Last off was Laura, the youthful glow all but gone from her twenty-nine-year-old face. The winter's wind tossed her long raven-black hair around like a child's plaything, blowing a cold breeze that found its way into her thin coat, chilling her very bones. She tucked a loose strand of hair behind her ear, unconcerned with concealing the large port wine stain birthmark covering her right hand that she'd come to accept as something that made her special. Maybe the only thing that made her special.

This is what it's come down to, she thought as she stepped onto the platform and the bus closed its doors behind her with a *hiss.*

She turned to the city, to the empty skyscrapers with their facades lit up as though they were their own beacons to tired travellers. Somewhere in the distance, several police sirens echoed out. Even closer still, she could hear two men yelling at one another, their words indistinguishable, but the animosity was there.

Just another night in the city.

Laura pulled her flimsy winter coat tighter around her body and stepped into the depot.

She tugged at the straps of her backpack as her footsteps echoed through the nearly-empty building. The other passengers had dispersed quickly, like cockroaches at the flicker of light. The yellow walls seemed to wilt under the fluorescent lights; the stench of old water and ripe bodies tickled her nose. The cheap fabric chairs, once a brightly patterned purple, now sat in shades of filth and rips.

Others sat scattered throughout the open space, all sitting far enough away from one another to avoid unnecessary contact. All were not there to catch a bus, but to sleep. When the area shelters were full, the depot turned a blind eye to those looking for somewhere warm for the night, especially in the winter.

Laura kept her gaze in front of her, not breaking even as she felt the eyes of the others shift to her. She knew better than to look at someone, especially at night, especially in this neighbourhood.

Rule number one in the city: don't make eye contact.

Laura had her list of do's and don't's, carefully constructed over a dozen or so visits. This wasn't her first time on the long-haul bus ride from her shitty small town, it wasn't even her tenth. She'd had lost count of how many times her mother, Mary, had disappeared in the middle of the night, often gone for days, weeks, or months at a time, only to randomly call one day asking for Laura to come down to the city and get her out of police custody or to send her some money or to pay her bus fare home. It was always one thing or another with Mary.

And Laura always answered, like the dutiful daughter she was. *Yes, mother. No, mother. How much do you need for drug money, mother?*

This time, though, this time felt different. This time *was* different. There was something in Mary's voice that sounded off in the message she had left, more off than normal.

"I wanted to say that I'm sorry and that you won't see me again," Mary had said. "I love you, Laura."

Laura had listened to the message a day after Mary had left it, unenthused to hear what her mother had to say. She'd called the unfamiliar number back right after hearing it, finding it was the Unity Mission Women's Shelter, a place that Mary haunted from time to time. The pleasant-sounding woman on the phone, Nancy, said she hadn't seen Mary in a while, but that she'd keep an eye out for her.

Laura had sworn up and down that she was through helping her mother, especially after her last trip to the city, where she'd found Mary, unresponsive, crumpled up on the floor in a meth house. The bus ride home had been long and painful. Mary had slept the whole way through, while Laura had sat next to her, watching her, hating her. Just because they were blood didn't mean that they were family. She was tired of the run-around. Tired of leaving her own sad life behind at a moment's notice to rescue the woman who should've been the one saving her. Tired of being the parent, even though she was on her way to thirty herself, an age that had been drilled into her head as the end-all. Movies and TV and magazines had said it: if you weren't married or had babies or a mortgage by thirty, then what good were you?

But all that hate, all that remorse, all that frustration went out the window when Mary uttered, "I love you, Laura"—words she'd never heard from her own mother's mouth.

That was how she knew something was wrong.

Laura reached the front sliding doors of the bus depot. She peered out the frost-covered glass—the streets weren't busy at this hour, she'd have no problem making her way to the police station to file a missing persons report, then she'd find somewhere to rest for the night. In the morning, she'd start searching.

For the last time, she thought as she stepped through the doors into the winter's chill. *Find her and bring her home, or leave her out here forever. There's no more after this.*

In the seating area, near the back of the rows where the reach of the fluorescent lights started to fade, sat a woman with a scarred face. A woman who glared at Laura from under the shadows of her black hood.

And as Laura ventured out into the darkness, the woman stood up and followed.

III

Cee sat on her mattress in her windowless room with her back against her single brick wall. A dull bulb shone an orange hue overhead, and the hallway light seeped through from under her metal door, reflecting off the three other metal walls. She'd found it nearly impossible to sleep with that crack of light in the beginning—always on for the worker bees, the lifeless drones who only lived to serve, and serve they did—but eventually, it became just as commonplace as the screaming or the metallic stench that lingered over every inch of this place.

She'd been one of them, once—a worker bee. A young girl cast out of her own home, looking for someone to love her. Someone to call her their own.

Before she knew it, her friends, who'd promised their couches and homes to her, had shut their doors and changed their locks and blocked their phone numbers. Her family, the few she could rely on, disappeared all the same. They blamed her for everything, they said that she'd made it all up, that she'd lied about it all. They said she was the toxic one. They said she had only done this to herself, that her mother was sick and not to blame.

So off she'd gone, no older than sixteen but thinking she

knew best, on her own. Thinking she could survive a life on the streets.

The first few months had been an adjustment—not knowing if she'd have a place to sleep, rationing her little food in case the usual dumpsters behind restaurants were picked over by the time she'd gotten there.

But she'd done it. She'd survived. She'd proven it to herself that she was a fighter, that she didn't need anyone or anything to protect her. She could take care of herself.

Still, she longed for a warm bed. And even more, though she'd never said it out loud, Cee longed for a mother. A *real* mother. One who would love her unconditionally; one who would take care of her; one that wouldn't hit her or stab her or burn her in spots hidden by her clothing.

Someone shuffled by her door then, their boots clinking against the metal floor. Above, the usual sounds of rattling pipes shook. She'd come to know every sound of this place, which they'd come to call the Underground, the clinks and clangs, the hours when most active. For an abandoned building, the old ghosts running through the pipes and walls kept busy at all hours.

Much farther up, out of her hole in the earth, it was almost night. Cee didn't get out much when the sun was out. She had a specific duty, one that required the veil of night, when she was free to leave, to roam the streets, almost carelessly through downtown, to do what she did best—hunt.

Cee gave her head a shake and sat up on her floor-level mattress. She looked to her metal walls, all three adorned with shelving, shelving filled to the brim with knickknacks and treasures and things she'd found on the streets, things tossed away like trash. The items on display gave her something to look forward to as she lay in bed, waiting for sleep to take her. She'd often look over one of her many trinkets, coming up with stories as to what they had meant to someone at one point in time, before they'd been forgotten, before they'd been left out to rot.

She turned to face her brick wall then, her fingers finding the fingertip-sized slits around one loose stone. She wiggled her fingers on either side of the slab, removing it from the wall, and reached her hand into the void.

She pulled out a vintage box, the logo and design just as worn as the pipes above her, the tin lid creaking as she carefully opened it.

Inside, a collection of trinkets and jewelry amassed over the years greeted her.

Her private treasures—things that meant something to her; things that needed to be guarded, hidden away.

Her pale finger pushed through each item, lingering on a few of them long enough to rouse a memory and a partial smile on her face—half a carnival ticket, an old high school football championship ring, a folded up newspaper article, and her latest piece: a golden locket.

Cee picked the necklace up, letting it twirl in her fingers. The light from under the door caught it as it spun, filling her room with a golden glow.

Cee stopped the spin, then placed the necklace around her. It dangled low, just around her heart. The metal felt cool against her chest.

Above her, the pipes sang their waking song as they pushed along the evening meal into everyone's rooms, through a small tube on the metal wall opposite Cee. She watched as a pile of gore seeped its way in through the round pipe cover, spilling into the feeding bucket below.

Not tonight, she thought as she stood, readying for what lay ahead.

Readying for the hunt.

IV

Laura sat upright in the hard plastic chair, feet tapping anxiously against the worn linoleum floor. The digital sign that hung from the ceiling had been flashing fifty-five for what seemed like an eternity. She looked down at the paper ticket in her hand: fifty-six.

Two police officers lounged at their desks like two balding overseers on the late-night shift, both uninterested in moving things along faster than necessary.

One officer was busy filling in a report by hand, taking his time with each and every letter that he penned. The other sat at his desk, punching at his computer keyboard with both hands, one index finger at a time.

At this rate, Laura *would* be there for eternity.

Her eyes rolled to the wall near the entrance of the station, the one littered with MISSING posters, some that she'd seen during her visits over the years, some as new as the past week. Almost all of them were women—the missing and murdered, those overlooked by the very people Laura sat in wait for, those whose cases would likely never be solved.

She hoped her mother would never be among them.

Still, her eyes scanned the photos from afar, thinking maybe someone—an acquaintance of her mother's; a concerned citizen— had come in before her to report Mary missing. Laura hoped Mary had someone like that here in the city, someone willing to search her out after a strange phone call, someone who hadn't seen her in a while, someone who was worried for her wellbeing.

But none of the posters were of Mary Harmon.

The station doors opened behind Laura. She cast a backward glance and saw a woman with a hood pulled over her head, obstructing the full view of her face. Laura could make out the shadows of several scars though, scars running across her mouth, her chin, and her cheeks.

The woman sat a few rows back from Laura. Laura tried to avert her gaze, but there was something about the woman's face that she couldn't turn away from. She wanted to see how far the scars travelled, she wanted to know how she'd gotten them.

The woman cocked her head in Laura's direction. And though she couldn't see exactly where the woman was staring, Laura knew she'd broken her own rule—don't make eye contact.

"Fifty-six."

Laura turned back to the officers. The digital sign now flashed her number.

The computer-typing cop coughed into the air, not bothering to shield anyone from his germs. He called out once more with a hurried impatience, as though he had more important things to do at three in the morning. "Fifty-six."

Laura grabbed her backpack and moved toward the officer, the woman's eyes following her as she walked.

The nameplate on the officer's messy desk read Sergeant Dick Fontaine. Laura sat down, eyes scanning the mountains of paperwork stained with old coffee rings and tiny crumbs from the overcooked bagel that he was currently shoving into his mouth.

Fontaine chewed, eyes still on the screen, freed fingers still typing one letter at a time.

"I'd like to—" Laura began.

"Just a minute," Fontaine interrupted, swallowing his bite. He pressed one final key, then turned to her, his glance giving her the once over, placing her in a box before she'd even stated her reason for being there.

"You good?" she asked, feeling the venom readying on her tongue. Fontaine simply stared.

"I'd like to report a missing person," Laura said.

Fontaine sighed and turned back to his computer. "Name."

"Hers or mine?"

"Yours first."

"Laura Harmon."

"Missing person."

"Mary Harmon."

"Relation."

Laura peered around his desk. Photos of him and what had to be his young grandkids were littered amongst the paperwork and crumpled McDonald's wrappers. Happy memories, taken at the lake, at Disneyland, at the park. She wished she had photos like that, as forced as some of them appeared. She didn't even know if a photo of her and Mary existed.

"She's my mother."

"When was the last time you saw her," Fontaine said, not asked, like he'd said it a million times before.

"I haven't seen her in a while."

"What's a while?"

Laura paced herself. "About a month. We don't . . . she left me a message a few days ago."

"So what makes you think she's missing?" An actual question. He leaned back in his chair, folding his thick arms across his protruding belly.

"She sounded strange, like she was in trouble. I could hear it in her voice."

Fontaine watched Laura, uncertainty in his eyes. "Did you call her back?"

"Yeah, but she wasn't there."

"She didn't answer her own phone?"

"No, she doesn't have a phone."

"So where does she usually call you from then?"

"From wherever she's staying," Laura said. She could feel the frustration rising inside her at the officer's stupid questions.

"A house? An apartment?"

"No, from a . . . "

"What?"

"A women's shelter."

Fontaine sat back up. His fat fingers finding the keyboard again. "What was your mother's name?"

"Mary Harmon."

Fontaine typed in Mary's name and hit enter. His eyes scanned the screen as her rap sheet populated. Laura leaned forward, over the debris, to see Mary's mugshot.

"Drug charges . . . breaking and entering . . . felony misdemeanor . . . your mom has quite the record."

Laura watched him as he read, trying her best to contain herself. She knew exactly where this conversation was headed.

It was the same place it always headed.

And it always ended the same.

"It looks like you've filed a few reports with us before."

"So?"

Fontaine stopped reading and leaned back in his chair once more.

"Have you checked the hospitals?"

"I've called them all—the hospitals, the shelters, the drunk tanks, the morgues, everything."

"And?"

Laura sighed. "And why else would I be here?"

"Listen, sweetie," Fontaine chastised, "I'm here to help you. No need to get all snarky with me."

Laura took a breath, bringing her hands together in her lap. She clenched one hand into a fist, letting her nails dig into the skin of her palm, focusing her growing rage into that one spot.

Don't snap don't snap don't—

"Call them again," he interrupted. "Go to her regular shelter and find someone who knows her. They can help you the most. You never know where people like your mom will show up."

Laura unclenched her fist. She glared at Fontaine. "People like my mom . . . what's that supposed to mean?"

"Look," Fontaine shrugged, the words having no significance to him. "There's nothing we can do at this point."

"What are you talking about?" Laura's voice grew. "She's a

missing person. I'm reporting her missing. Are you refusing to take this seriously?"

"Listen, sweetheart, I've seen this a million times before. In most cases, these people pop up after a few days—"

"Jesus Christ, I'm telling you she's in trouble!"

Laura shot up from the chair. She could feel the heat inside growing, the pent-up rage and anger ready to boil over. They never listened, the police. No matter how much she screamed or remained calm, the answer was always the same.

"Sit down," Fontaine motioned at Laura. "This isn't helping your case."

"I want to talk to your supervisor."

"I am the supervisor."

"I want to talk to *your* supervisor."

Fontaine rolled his eyes and expelled a bagel-filled breath. "He's at home, in his bed, sleeping soundlessly because he doesn't have to work the overnight shift."

"I don't give a fuck. Wake him up."

Fontaine eyed Laura once more, the small cogs in his brain debating on how to get rid of Laura as quickly as possible. Even the other cop, still carefully filling out his report like he was penning an ancient text, had turned his attention to them.

"Your mom's probably in a drunk tank at another station. Ask around. Someone's seen her."

"I just told you I've done all that. And that's your job. Not mine."

"Ma'am, please calm down."

Laura glared at the man, incredulous. "So you're not going to help me?"

"Start at the shelter. Work your way from there. If you still haven't found her in a few days, come back, then we'll talk. But I guarantee she's out there trying to score drugs."

Fontaine pressed a button on his desk. The digital number flipped from fifty-six to fifty-seven. Laura turned to the row of chairs—there was no one else waiting.

She spun back to Fontaine. He kept his eyes on his computer, closing Mary's rap sheet, a losing game of Solitaire now filling the screen.

"If you don't help me," Laura started, pointing to the wall of missing posters, "she's going to end up like everyone else on that wall. And that'll be on your hands."

Fontaine's eyes flickered to the wall, then back to his screen.

"There's nothing I can do right now, sweetheart," he said, his voice emotionless. "My hands are tied."

Laura shoved the station doors open and stormed outside. It had started to snow, just a little, but enough to cover the icy streets in an undisturbed light white coat.

Laura swung her backpack off her shoulder and dug through it, going for her phone. She pulled it out, tucking her backpack on the ground between her boots. She held her phone in front of her, the screen's light shining on her face and casting a glow back into the vestibule behind her, where the hooded woman stood, watching Laura from behind the glass.

Laura needed to rest, to let her boiling blood simmer before going out and searching. Her anger, one of the few qualities she'd picked up from Mary, had been nothing but a hindrance to her personal life. It had ruined relationships, both platonic and not; it had left its mark on others, some permanently so; it made her brash and unforgiving and impulsive in the best and the worst of times.

It was something that she learned to control, albeit a little. Old Laura would've shoved Fontaine's papers off his desk. Old Laura would've taken his family photos and thrown them to the ground. Old Laura would've used her fists instead of her words, because Old Laura knew they got the quickest response.

But Old Laura was a quiet partner now, someone who only tried to break loose when the moment felt right. She hadn't been out in quite some time. New Laura had seen to it.

A park would do for the night, she decided. All the shelters were closed for the night, likely at full capacity, as usual. It wouldn't be the first time she'd huddled underneath a bench for an hour or two, and she'd come prepared for the occasion—an extra layer of clothing and a large, warm blanket would keep her insulated for now. Then, first thing tomorrow, she'd find the Unity Mission Women's Shelter, Mary's last known whereabouts.

She pulled out her map and looked up nearby parks as the door to the police station swung open behind her. She inched off to the side without raising her head, her backpack still nestled at her feet.

Laura looked up in time to see the hooded woman slowly pass by, then suddenly lean back.

The woman grabbed Laura's backpack and took off down the street.

"Hey!" Laura shouted, shoving her map into her pocket. "Stop!"

She darted after the figure, throwing caution to the wind on the icy sidewalks.

Her whole life was in that bag—forty dollars, her ID, and the only photo she had of Mary. She couldn't let it go.

"Stop!"

The woman ran fast.

But Laura kept on her.

Deeper they sprinted into the city, deeper into the concrete jungle where it was easy to get lost, to take a misstep, to wind up somewhere you shouldn't be, until they turned into a part of town that Laura didn't recognize, one littered with brutalist-style buildings, with broken windows and boarded-up doorways, with flat stone facades that had a sharpness about them, a meanness.

The woman turned a tight corner then, agile on her feet as though she'd ran this same route a million times before.

And when Laura turned the corner herself, coming face to face with a dead end, she realized the woman had, in fact, done this a million times before.

She'd been led into a back alley.

She'd been led into a trap.

Multiple boots crunched on the fresh snow behind her. Laura turned, seeing two other figures blocking her exit. Laura tensed, but turned back to the hooded woman, who rested with her back against the far stone wall.

"Just give me my backpack and I'll walk away. You don't need to do anything stupid here."

The woman held Laura's backpack out, taunting her like a schoolyard bully. Then, she tossed it to the side, its contents spilling out onto the trash- and dirt-filled snow.

They don't want my stuff, Laura thought. *They want something else.*

Laura slowly put her hands into her coat pockets, trying not to raise any sort of alarm with her assailants.

"I'm trying to find my mom. Can I show you a picture? Maybe you've seen her."

The woman eyed her from under her hood. She could feel the glares of the others on her back.

Inside one pocket, Laura's fingers found what they were looking for.

Laura took a step toward the woman and pulled out her hands.

The woman cocked her head downward, lining up perfectly with Laura's pepper spray.

Another one of Laura's rules—*always be ready to defend yourself.*

The hooded woman screamed as the liquid met her eyes, sending her stumbling to the ground. The scream was unlike anything Laura had ever heard.

It was guttural. Animal-like. Unnatural.

Before Laura had a chance to make a run for it, the two others were on her.

They threw her to the ground, knocking the breath out of her chest, sending the spray flying from her hands. They held her arms down with so much force, Laura thought her bones would snap.

She screamed into the night as she watched the hooded woman step toward her, her hood now down, exposing her features under a sliver of light from the street beyond. She was no older than Laura. Brown hair as long as hers. Eyes so pale of a blue, it was almost as though they were white. The scars Laura had thought she saw at the police station were nothing more than uneven patches of skin, colours different than her actual skin tone, as though she were a living, breathing mosaic and her face was the artboard.

She looked like a modern-day Frankenstein's monster.

Laura screamed again. She screamed to the street, her cries falling upon an empty city. She kicked and thrashed and tried to break free from the grip of the other two, but it was useless.

Then, the hooded woman kicked her across the face.

The sounds of the city faded away, replaced by a high-pitched ringing.

Lights flickered and pulsed.

Snow drifted upwards and downwards.

Laura tried with every fibre of her being to maintain consciousness. She could feel herself slipping away, down into the darkness where it was warm. Where it was safe.

She watched the woman float to her stomach, lifting her coat to her chest. Then, she could only feel pressure. Pressure and warmth, like the woman had thrown Laura into the river and was pushing her down to the riverbed.

Slowly, the warmth turned into burning, as though Laura's own rage had manifested into a real thing and was spilling from her insides.

The other two released her arms and went to join in with their leader, snapping at one another with guttural clicks.

Laura's head fell to the side as blood began to pool around her. She spotted her backpack, her wallet, the single photo of Mary, all scattered about.

And nestled among them, her pepper spray.

It was within arms' reach.

Laura stretched toward it, unsure if there was any strength left in her to give. Unsure if her torso wouldn't come apart at the middle if she reached too far.

Her fingertips grasped at the small cannister.

But they only pushed it farther away.

Laura opened her mouth, a final scream building in her throat.

But only blood spilled out.

She could feel the heaviness in her eyes, the darkness even darker now, the sounds of the splashing liquid fading away.

But somewhere in the alley, another figure moved about.

There was a sudden lightness around Laura's abdomen.

Laura watched in half-consciousness as two bodies flew into the sky, like two birds ready to soar.

Then the bodies hit the ground, hard, shattering their bones and cracking their jaws in a way that made them look like they were now stuck in an eternal scream.

The hooded woman stood up, facing a darkened corner of the dead end, Laura's blood dripping from her mouth like a cold drink on a hot summer's day.

As Laura battled the darkness, she caught the hooded woman saying, "—mistake."

Then, the hooded woman ran off, scurrying like a scared child into the night.

The new figure, a woman, came to Laura, kneeling down beside her, a pale face with dark eyes, dark eyes that looked like long-extinguished embers.

The last thing Laura saw before fading off was the glint of a golden necklace dangling above her.

V

The sounds of rush hour traffic flooded into Laura's ears, the honks and shouts of the city, muffled by the off-white walls that made up the large room she found herself in. Fluorescent lights buzzed above; a stale air hung around her like a cloud.

She sat up, stiff, but still intact. Her body buzzed with the memory of last night, a stinging around her abdomen that she dared not look at.

She did look about, though—two purple half walls flanked either side of the small room she'd been brought to, one wall near the cot she was resting on, the other near a second cot, empty, already made for the day. Two nightstands were placed beside each bed, with a standing mirror nestled between them. Above her, fastened to the wall, were cubby holes for storage. At the foot of her bed, resting on a chest, was her backpack, her clothes washed and folded neatly next to it.

Laura moved her legs to the side of the bed and took her time standing up, shaky, grunting at the discomfort in her belly. The small half-room she was in was part of a much larger building that stretched a good length—there had to be at least twenty beds, all on one side of the room with a makeshift path on the other, one way leading to the front of the building and the other way leading to what looked like an office in the back. She scratched at the long T-shirt that someone had put on her, one that hung loosely against her skin.

Laura grabbed her backpack, sitting back down on the flimsy cot, the springs poking at her skin. She rummaged through, finding everything was still there. Her pepper spray, her money, the only photo of Mary that she had.

Someone had cleaned it up.

Someone had brought her here.

A sudden knock on the half-wall startled her. Laura spun around to see a tall woman around sixty watching her from behind golden-rimmed glasses. Her outfit, though homely, looked too baggy for her small frame.

"I'm so glad you're up, Laura," the woman smiled. She took a cautious step inward as Laura pushed over on the bed, unsure. "I'm Nancy. We spoke a few days ago, on the phone. About your mother." Nancy extended a wrinkled hand to Laura.

"Nice to meet you," Laura said, returning the greeting and relaxing a little. "Sorry, but . . . how did I get here?"

Nancy's smile didn't falter. "I was hoping you could tell me that. I found you by the back door, crumpled on the ground. You were in pretty rough shape. Looked like someone had . . . well, it looked worse than it actually was."

"It did?"

"Yeah, your shirt and coat were soaked. I thought you'd been stabbed, but when I took a look for myself, you seemed fine. What happened to you?"

Nancy eyed Laura with a cautious look. Laura struggled to find the words to say, to tell this woman that she'd been attacked by three women with fucked up faces, and that, in theory, she should have a gaping wound in her stomach that, from the way it had felt last night, should've killed her.

But Laura had another rule that she lived by in the city, one to follow for now until she knew for certain that Nancy was an ally—*trust no one.*

"Do you remember anything at all?" Nancy pried again.

"It's . . . a little fuzzy," Laura said.

Nancy put a sympathetic hand on her shoulder. "It doesn't really matter anyway. I'm not here to ask questions, just to help. I cleaned the blood off you the best I could, washed your clothes, then got you settled for the night. I hope you don't mind."

"No," Laura managed. "I . . . thank you."

"Of course," Nancy smiled. "I help all the women that come to Unity Mission."

Laura fumbled for her backpack, pulling out the photo of Mary, a much younger version of her, long before Laura had been the mistake that she'd opted to keep. "When we spoke, you said you'd seen my mom, right?"

Laura passed the photo to Nancy, who took it into her wrinkled hands. She studied it with more grace and compassion than the cop. "Yes, of course. Mary Harmon. My, she's so young here. She's beautiful."

Laura's eyes lit up. "Are you sure that's the woman you saw?"

Nancy studied the image a moment more. "I never forget a

face," she said, passing the photo back, Nancy's gaze now falling upon Laura's features, as though seeing her for the first time. "You look like her. Same young eyes. Same soft skin."

"Do you have any idea where she is?" Laura asked, putting the picture into her backpack.

"No, honey."

"Did you notice anything off about her? Anything strange?"

"No . . ." Nancy hesitated, lowering her voice. "Well . . . "

Laura took a breath and stood up. "Please, any information you have will help. I need to find my mom."

"What you need is rest," Nancy said, matter-of-factly.

Laura felt the fire then, the tickle of Old Laura asking to come out and play. Who did Nancy think she was, trying to tell Laura what to do? Laura clenched one of her fists, digging her nails into her hand, channeling it away. The fire started to fade.

"I'm going out to find her," she said, calmly. "I've already lost too much time."

Laura grabbed her pants and pulled them on, her belly still a little tender. It didn't matter, though. None of it mattered, not the pain, not Nancy who'd seemed so willing to help on the phone. Laura would do this on her own, like she always had. Mary was out there somewhere. It would just take a little more time to bring her home.

Finally, Nancy sighed. "You're just like Mary, you know—tenacious. Strong-willed."

Laura threw on her freshly laundered coat, the clean scent of dryer sheets biting at the stale air, hands digging into her pockets—the pepper spray was in its place.

"She was hanging out with a woman who lives in the industrial part of town," Nancy said, a firmness in her voice. "A tall woman, with short hair and . . . distinct features."

"Does this woman have a name?"

Nancy seemed to hesitate once more, but muttered, "Cee."

"Got it." That was more than enough for Laura to go on.

"You need to be careful, Laura."

"Mmhmm." Laura's mind was only focused on one thing now: Mary.

"I mean it. A lot of young women go missing around here."

"I appreciate your concern, really, but this isn't the first time I've had to pull Mary out of a bad situation."

Nancy stood up. "I'm sorry to hear that."

"You and me both."

"Listen," Nancy said, stopping Laura before she exited her room. "We're below capacity so you can stay here while you look. But in exchange, I'll need you to do something for me."

"What do you need?"

Nancy smiled. "Let's talk tomorrow. Curfew's at ten tonight. Be back by then."

"I will, thank you."

Nancy nodded one last time before leaving Laura's space.

Laura watched the woman shuffle down the hall to the back of the shelter. She took small, child-like steps that made her seem uncomfortable in her own skin.

Laura turned back to her area, making sure she had everything that she needed. Her gaze found her reflection in the mirror, a woman she barely recognized staring back at her.

Her face was bruised, a little swollen. Her long black hair tussled and knotted.

Laura inhaled. She had to see what'd been done to her. A visit to the hospital wasn't ideal, but she'd regret not going if the wound became infected, or something worse.

Slowly, Laura pulled the T-shirt up and the waistband of her pants down, wincing at the strange feeling in abdomen.

She looked away, bracing herself for the damage done. She expected a roughly sewed gash, a scene of pure carnage.

But when her eyes finally found her stomach, there was no wound.

No gaping maw.

No roughly sewed gash.

There was only skin.

Discoloured.

Patchy.

As though someone had sewn her back together.

Like the face of the woman who'd attacked her.

VI

When Laura checked the time on her dying phone, it was quarter to ten.

She wasn't anywhere near the shelter. There was no way she'd make curfew. She was exhausted, and not just from the lingering mysteries of why her wound was already healed or the identity of the person who'd saved her. Her exhaustion sprang from her fight against the remaining daylight, sprinting across the industrial part of town, looking for anyone who fit Nancy's description: Cee, a tall woman, with distinct features. She hadn't pressed on the definition of 'distinct,' but she felt in her gut that she already knew what it meant.

This woman was someone who looked like her attackers.

Laura had squandered enough time roaming derelict buildings and empty relics, and all for nothing. No one lived in or around the area, there were no residences nearby and all the factories had been long shut down. The area, with its imposing ruins, its shuttered doors, its crumbling brick faces, was a whisper of what it used to be, a ghost town in the heart of the city.

She'd been vigilant in her searching, taking time as she walked through abandoned factories to call the same shelters, the same hospitals, the same morgues as the day before, all for the same news.

She took it for what it was worth: neither good nor bad.

Mary was still out there, somewhere.

Laura sprinted again now, checking the time once more. 9:55. And with that final use of power, the screen on her phone went black, the dead battery symbol flashing in a sort of mockery. She was closer to the shelter, but not close enough. And now, she had no way of contacting Nancy to let her know.

Laura came to a short tunnel that passed under some raised train tracks, a sketchy, orange-lit road allowing passage from the industrial area into downtown. Laura considered her options—the raised tracks seem to go on forever in either direction, and she was long past her original entry point. There didn't seem to be any other way around the tracks. She had to go through the tunnel.

It gave her solace, seeing the other side of the street a few yards up, a signal to a false sense of safety. As quickly as she moved, she pushed a little more to not linger in the tunnels' many shadows.

Until she saw the mural.

She came up on it at its far end, hand painted imagery of what looked like rocks growing in size. Slowly, the rocks morphed into faces—anguished faces, pained faces, faces of women, dead-eyed and haunted. Hundreds of them, if not more.

Laura slowed her pace, suddenly infatuated with the art

before her. There was something about them that she couldn't look away from.

She followed the faces through the orange light, more and more of them in different pained expressions, until the reach of the light faded, casting the rest of the mural in heavy darkness. It continued on—she could see the faces spreading out, giving way to something . . . some*one* . . . else.

Laura swung her backpack in front of her and knelt down. She searched through its contents until she found her flashlight.

The stark white light obliterated any hint of the orange hue, showing off every intended stroke of the paintbrush, every harsh line of the spray paint can.

Laura's eyes followed the faces to their end, their expressions growing more and more distorted, their faces blending together like patchwork.

And there, standing above the others, was the full-bodied painting of a woman.

Jagged lines cut across her skin like the Frankensteined faces of Laura's assaulters, like Laura's own stomach, the woman's body a tapestry of colours. Her face was old, withered. Her eyes looked human, but one who'd seen many sunrises and sunsets. She had no nose, only tiny vertical slits where her nostrils should be, which led down to her lips, the skin coming together in bunches and folds as though she hadn't had a sip of water in centuries. Her face was both beautiful and obscene. On her head, she wore a golden crown, one that seemed to shimmer in the strength of the flashlight.

And underneath her, a name had been scrawled in bold, black letters.

Mother.

It was 10:12 when Laura ran up to Unity Mission's doors. They'd been long locked, the remnants of any inside light extinguished.

"Shit," she murmured to herself, pounding on the glass. "Nancy! Hello?"

No one answered her call.

Laura turned and faced the empty street, keeping her back pressed against the shuttered doors as she slipped to the ground. From under the building's overhang, a light snow had started to come down, blending with the other snow from storms passed. She pulled her thin coat a little tighter and shivered. She could go back to the industrial area and find somewhere to hunker down for the night. That would also give her the chance to keep an eye out for the woman, as long as she stayed awake. She would continue again in the morning. Not as fresh-eyed as she intended, but still awake and alive and determined to bring Mary home.

"Hey."

Laura snapped toward the voice, her hands instantly going into her coat pockets.

A tall woman approached her.

"Are you . . . okay?"

Laura stood up, one hidden hand gripping her pepper spray, her finger on the trigger. "Yeah. I just . . . got locked out for the night."

The woman stood a few inches taller than her. She had old scars across her face that only seemed to accentuate her features, and short hair that framed her androgynous face.

Laura was immediately infatuated and suddenly aware of her own messy appearance. She shifted a little, straightening out the bumps in her coat.

"Nancy's a stickler for curfew," the woman said, eying Laura with the same curiosity. "I know a place you can stay for the night. It isn't much, but it's safe. And warm."

"Oh, uh . . . " a million excuses raced through Laura's mind. She didn't want to come across rude, a trait built-in to most women who were taught at a young age to always be agreeable, even if the situation was uncomfortable. But, at the same time, there was something about her that put Laura at ease. The woman knew Nancy, or, at least, Nancy's name. There was something trustworthy about her. Something familiar. Was this the woman Nancy had mentioned? Did she know where Mary was?

"Sorry, I'm not a creep or anything, I swear," the woman smirked, as though reading Laura's mind. "You know what, you look hungry. Why don't we go grab something to eat instead?"

Laura's self-imposed rules flashed before her eyes—*don't make eye contact, trust no one, always be ready to defend yourself*—but a restaurant was a public place. If things went south, at least there would be other people around.

"Okay, sure," Laura said, waiting for the woman to take the

lead. This was the woman Nancy had mentioned. She had to be. "I'm Laura, by the way."

The woman glanced at Laura with her dark eyes, eyes that looked like two extinguished embers. "Cee."

VII

They spent most of the night at Frankie's Diner, a 24-hour dive not far from the Mission.

Cee would never admit it out loud, but she loved it at Frankie's. Something about its kitschy décor and greasy surfaces made her feel at home. She came in at least three times a week—even more during the winter—to take a break from hunting. There was only so much she could do in a night, and lately, she'd been less inspired to get her work done.

She'd been doing this same song and dance for as long as she could remember. At first, it had been thrilling, luring the unaware to the Underground, seeing their expressions as she brought them into different rooms for different purposes—sometimes it was the waiting room, when Mother wanted to test the gumption of new initiates; other times it was straight to Mother's chamber, for her own enjoyment; and sometimes, on the rarest of occasions, it was to the room on the bottom floor, the room where the transformations took place.

Cee had liked watching the roaming souls meet their ends. She'd liked being first in command, overseeing several others to help recruit and feed the members of their community. She'd liked being near the head of the table when it came time to feast (after Mother, of course), but the communal dinners had been a thing of the past. Now, they all kept to themselves, those in the Underground, their meals suctioned through old metal pipes and deposited into their rooms for them to feast alone, in the dark.

It had once been all so new. So fun.

Now, she felt trapped.

She wanted out.

Cee watched Laura as she ate with ferocity, pushing her long black hair behind her ears with a hand covered in a port wine stain birthmark, a muted red that made Cee think of a crushed strawberry both in shape and in colour. Her soft, warm-hued skin seemed to glow in the harsh lights of the diner, her youthful brown eyes growing more and more satiated with every bite. Cee had never seen anyone quite like her.

"You're not eating?" Laura asked, mouth full of a club sandwich and Frankie's signature curly fries.

"Not hungry."

Laura shrugged and went back to her meal, stuffing more ketchup-soaked fries into her mouth. Cee inhaled, the memory of salt on her tongue. She couldn't remember how long it had been since she'd eaten anything other than what was fed to her.

"So," Cee started, fiddling with a sugar pack. "You said your mom's missing?"

Laura nodded, swallowing her mouthful. "Yeah, I came down here to find her. Here—"

Laura wiped her hands on her napkin, then dug through her backpack. She pulled out a photo and passed it to Cee. "Have you seen her? It's an old photo, but she still looks the same."

Cee looked it over. She couldn't say for sure. She'd seen hundreds, maybe even thousands, of women in her lifetime who'd looked as beautiful as young Mary once, but who now looked like another person entirely.

"No," she said, not wanting to give Laura any false hope. "That's . . . " In the second it took to say the word, Cee became blissfully aware of her lack of conversation skills. It'd been a long time since she'd even sat down with someone just to talk. So why now? Why Laura? " . . . that's really nice of you. Coming down here to look for her, I mean." Cee felt her insides heat up as she passed the photo back to Laura, their fingers touching for the briefest of moments, Laura's warmth lingering against Cee's cold skin. Laura didn't seem to notice.

"What's your story?" Laura asked, putting the photo away and taking another bite of her sandwich, an off look in her eyes.

"My story?"

"Yeah, how'd you end up out here? What's your deal?"

"I've been out here a while," Cee started. "Home wasn't great, so I split. Luckily, I found someone to take me in."

"So you don't live on the streets?"

"I mean . . . " Cee thought of the best way to describe her situation. "It's complicated."

Laura nodded, trying to piece Cee's story together. "But you've been out here a long time, right? You know the streets pretty well?"

"Mmhmm."

"What do you know about a painting under the train tracks? It has a monster on it, a monster called Mother."

"That's . . . just a mural," Cee said. She looked up and met Laura's eyes. "There's a ton of them around the city."

There had been many, at one point, back in the earlier days when Mother had been nothing more than a rumour, a whisper in the night. It had been one of Cee's many jobs to go paint over any that appeared. She knew the one Laura was talking of, the sea of faces, the exaggerated view of Mother, and she'd told Mother that she'd taken care of it. But when Cee had come face to face with that painting, she couldn't will herself to cover it.

She left it up, not as an invitation, but as a warning.

"Right," Laura said, eating the last fries on her plate. She sat back in the vinyl booth and heaved a sigh, checking the clock on the wall. "Well."

"Well?"

"It's only four. What do we do now?" Laura gave the faintest of smiles.

"Why don't we walk around a bit?" Cee said. "See if we can find other people who may have seen your mom."

Laura looked outside. The snow had stopped, but the streets were thick with ice. "I've already had some trouble out there. I don't want anymore."

Cee had wondered if Laura knew who she was, if she'd recognized her from the previous night. She'd arrived in the nick of time, following a scent that had been unfamiliar to her. A sickly-sweet smell, one that had immediately taken to her when her hunt had begun.

She had followed it to the outskirts of her area, to where Mother's outliers dwelled, the deformed women of the Underground who'd been exiled for disobeying, for breaking the chain of command.

Cee often let them go about their own business, sticking more to the core, but that scent—Laura's scent—had been intoxicating. Even more so when the three women tore her open.

She'd been tempted to join them, to take a meal for herself rather than bring something back for Mother to devour first, then toss her scraps to her loyal followers. But there'd been something in Laura's eyes as she'd looked up to the stars, as she took her last breaths, something that sparked a fire in Cee.

Cee forced a smile. "No one's going to bother you if you're out there with me."

The women spent the hours into dawn walking and talking. Cee had never felt so comfortable with someone she'd just met, someone as warm as Laura, someone she felt she could talk to about anything. Almost anything.

As the clocks rolled around to seven, they found themselves back at the Unity Mission, planning to meet up again that night for more searching.

An uneager Nancy unlocked the vestibule doors, glaring at Cee as Laura looked on.

"Go get some rest," Cee said, pulling her hood over her head to block out the rising sun. "Let's meet up again later."

"Okay," Laura said. "It was nice to have someone to walk with. Especially in the dark."

Cee smirked, casting one last glance at Nancy, who disapprovingly let Laura into the building.

As Laura disappeared into the shadows of the Mission, Nancy turned to Cee.

"You keep away from her," Nancy's voice was cold and harsh. They hadn't spoken since Nancy had opened the shelter all those years before; they'd only seen each other in passing. But the way some of the women in the Underground spoke of Nancy, of how much they missed her, of how kind and gentle she could be, Cee didn't recognize any of those features in this woman who stood before her, this woman with old, deep-set eyes and an irritated tone.

Cee gave Nancy one last look, then turned on her heels, heading back to the Underground, back to home.

Just before they'd reached the shelter doors, Laura had pried more about the mural, about the woman at its end. Cee could already tell that Laura's curiosity was limitless, that no doubt that trait had gotten her into trouble on more than one occasion. But Cee kept her cards close to her chest—if she mentioned the Underground, if she told Laura of a place where women went to disappear (and that Cee helped those women disappear, but was now trying to get herself away from it), she would know that Mary was there.

As they'd walked, Cee had kept the image of Mary in her mind, scanning through all the faces she'd seen over the past few days.

And by the time they returned to the shelter, Cee was sure of it—she'd led Mary straight to Mother.

VIII

"What were you doing with her?" Nancy voice suddenly filled Laura's small room as she removed her coat.

Laura turned to Nancy, not about to be intimidated. "I missed curfew last night and she offered to help."

"I told you to be careful, Laura."

"Look, I appreciate the hospitality, but I know what I'm doing. I can handle myself."

Nancy eyed Laura. "Can you?"

The words stung Laura, like the lashings Mary used to give her after she'd had a few too many. Laura grabbed her toothbrush and pushed by Nancy, moving to the bathroom. "I need to rest. I've been up all night."

"Wait a second," Nancy called out after her. "I want to show you something."

Laura followed Nancy into her office, a small room at the back of the shelter in pure organized chaos. Her computer was covered with sticky notes, looking more like a neon rainbow than a monitor. Her old metal desk was just as dinged up as the rest of the shelter, with papers and pens strewn about. The lights above seemed to buzz even louder in the contained space, their harsh glare unrelenting on each and every surface.

But what Nancy had strung up against her far wall caught Laura's attention.

It was wall plastered with the same missing posters from the police station.

Only, with more.

A lot more.

"Jesus," Laura muttered as she stepped closer to the posters. "Are all these women missing?"

"Yes," Nancy came up beside her, admiring her work, in a way. "Did you know them?"

"Every single one. I never forget a face. These women bounced around a lot, from shelter to shelter, but you hear things, working in the community for as long as I have. Once they stop visiting the places they used to or seeing people they associate with, it's clear that something's happened."

"So how do you know they didn't just go home or skip town?"

"They didn't have anywhere else to go."

"No family?"

"Just me," Nancy said. "These women have no one in their lives who care for them the way you do for your mom. Looking for them is the least I can do. To show them that I haven't forgotten."

"Did you try the police?"

"They're useless."

"Tell me about it," Laura chuckled, taking in all the faces. Every last one of them. "What have you found out?"

Nancy looked over at Laura. "A name. One that everyone seems to know, but no one ever talks about."

"Who?"

Nancy moved to her office door, her back to Laura, to close it. Laura watched as she did, noticing a wet spot of red on the back of her sweater.

"I asked you for a favour yesterday," Nancy said, closing the door gently. "And now I need your discretion, too. Your new friend knows about all these women. She may not be forthcoming about it, but she knows."

"What? How?"

"Cee lives in the Underground."

"What's the Underground?"

"It's where all these women are. It's where women in a rough spot can go under the guise of being safe. Of being loved. Of disappearing from the outside world. It's place where you have to pay a hefty price to get into . . . something that these women don't take into consideration until it's too late. Cee lives there, I know that much for sure." Nancy paused, taking a breath. "I think your mom might be in there, too. That's why I had to lock you out last night. I knew Cee would find you. She's always around here, looking for new recruits."

"You set me up?" Laura asked, noticing her rage not making its presence known. She'd been duped by Nancy, set up to find Cee. Yet, she wasn't angry. She wasn't even hurt. If anything, she was intrigued. What game were these two playing? And how was Mary involved?

"I'm sorry, it was the only way I could think of."

Laura turned back to Nancy, Mary's voicemail playing over and over again in her head. "You said the Underground is somewhere people go to disappear. When my mom called . . . it sounded like she was saying goodbye."

Nancy nodded, understanding.

"So how do I get there?"

"That's the favour I wanted to ask. I've never been able to find it. I need you to find out through Cee."

"You want me to use her."

"Cee isn't as innocent as she's led you to believe. That woman's been around a long time. Longer than I've been here. I know this is dangerous. I know I'm asking a lot of you, but right now, you're the only way in. If Cee's warming to you, she'll take you there."

Laura considered her options. "You're sure my mom's down there?"

Nancy nodded once more, confident in her answer.

Laura plopped herself down onto an old chair, giving herself a moment to take it all in. She thought Mary had overdosed or was in some trash house or maybe even living a better life out in the city with a secret family. She never considered was that her mother would join some sort of weird underground cult, all in the name of disappearing. Nancy watched her with a curious eye. Laura ran her hands through her hair.

"A name," Laura said. "You said you had a name."

"Yes, the woman who runs the Underground," Nancy replied. "Her name's Mother."

IX

Cee walked with her hands in her pockets, her face held high. She hadn't felt this way in a long time. If at all.

There was something about Laura that she couldn't shake. She felt drawn to her. She felt like she needed her, and that Laura needed her too.

Maybe this was her way out.

The thought crossed her mind as she passed into the industrial area, a place where not even the rats bothered to dwell. At the beginning, when Mother had found her and promised her a better life, they'd spent a lot of time in other areas thinking they'd be safe. And for a while, they were, but it wasn't long before the city showed its true colours. Heritage buildings, ones where they often found themselves hiding, were bought and sold like a game of Monopoly. The buildings they'd hidden in, slept in, feasted in, had all been slated for destruction, with condos and leisure centres going up in their place.

Cee would watch from a safe distance when the buildings were destroyed. And when their stones came crashing down, when their history went up in a cloud of dust, a piece of her crumbled along with them.

As her and Mother moved about, they finally came across the industrial sector, long abandoned and untouched due to soil contamination. It wasn't long before they'd found the Underground, an abandoned metal factory with an underground area that spanned multiple sublevels, large enough to house hundreds of souls.

That's when Mother had shared her plan with Cee—working together, they'd offer women a safe place to live. A place where she would make them all like her—eternal and undying—where they wouldn't have to worry about the dangers of living on the streets or the dangers of other people. They would all have each other and no one else. They would be a family.

And the cost? Not much, according to Mother. Just a lifelong commitment to keeping her safe and fed and alive. It was a small price to pay for safety. At least, Cee had thought so at the time.

Cee's bootsteps echoed down the hallway, she stepped over old papers, over broken glass, over torn up carpet. Up ahead, the dim light behind the weak wooden door beckoned her closer and closer. That light had once made her feel warm, alive even, and beyond that light, the women who longed to join their coven, knowing what was being asked of them, but never truly understanding until they were faced with their first task.

Once word had spread of a new safe place, they had to use the old manager's office to hold the women back. Cee wanted to let them all in, to give them all a chance at a better life, but Mother had been strict with her rules. They had to perform two tasks to prove their loyalty. And if they couldn't . . . they already knew too much. Mother didn't want word spreading even quicker than it already had, so she instructed Cee to bite it off at its head, so to speak. If someone failed the first initiation, they would be put to other uses.

But if they proved themselves, then they were welcomed into the Underground for the second trial by fire—an offering. Mother loved collecting trinkets—a trait passed down to Cee—items of special meaning to those who longed to follow her. By committing themselves to the Underground was to forget who you were on the outside world, so all your possessions, no matter how personal, had to be given to Mother, with the most valuable offered to her as the final sacrifice. Everyone who had passed through the rusted metal door had done it, including Cee. Though she'd long forgotten what her offering had been.

Cee opened the door to the waiting room. The three remaining women quickly found their footing and stood up.

But Cee moved straight to the door, not bothering to share a word with any of them.

"No one today?" one of them asked.

Cee stopped in her tracks. She looked at the women, two of them with their eyes downcast, but one, one stared at her dead-on. Cee stepped up to the woman. The others cowered back, but this one didn't. She licked at her lips.

There was hunger in the woman's eyes, and pain. Cee knew the look well. She had worn it herself for many years.

"You'll get your chance. Have patience."

The woman nodded. Cee could tell she was frustrated, that she wanted to say more, but she'd used up her adrenalin asking Cee the one question. All that was left in her eyes was fear. The same fear that fell upon everyone when they looked at Cee.

Everyone except Laura.

Cee glanced at each of them, filthy and sleep-deprived and shivering in the cold. They longed for something. They longed for hope. For shelter. For somewhere to belong—the things Cee had once longed for.

Only now that she had them, she didn't want them anymore.

X

When Cee arrived at the Unity Mission that night, Laura was nowhere to be found.

Cee waited for the better part of an hour, keeping away from the shelter's doors in case Nancy spotted her.

When it was obvious that Laura had left, Cee wandered around town, looking for any signs of her. But there were none to be found.

As curfew hit the Unity Mission once more, Cee made her way back to the Underground, to rest a little before the hunt, dejected and alone. Cee chided herself. She never should've left Laura's side. She should've kept her close. Kept her away from Nancy. No doubt that woman had something to do with Laura's absence.

The snow crunched under Cee's boots as she walked up Main Street, taking a hard left into the industrial area, her mind racing with a million thoughts as to where Laura was.

Sirens blared in the distance as Laura watched Cee walk through the decay of the industrial area. Graffitied walls and broken windows greeted her as she stayed as far back as she could without losing her trail.

She'd been watching Cee since she'd arrived, from the Mission's back lane. Laura assumed Cee would've given up after an hour of being shafted, but she'd stood there, waiting, for nearly three hours. Standing out in the cold that long had rendered Laura frozen.

Laura wanted to trust Cee, but there was something off about her, just like there was something off about Nancy. It might have been nothing between the both of them, but the one thing Laura trusted more than anything was her gut, and though she'd shunned it the other night after being locked out of the shelter, after spending the night with Cee, her gut was now screaming at her to listen to her rules.

But her heart was screaming louder, and it was calling Mary's name. She needed answers, and Cee had them.

Cee kicked at the snow as she walked, turning into the open, gaping maw of the ruins of an old factory that Laura hadn't searched. The building looked dangerous—the roof had long caved in, the windows long broken, even the ghosts that may have haunted it had long moved on. Laura picked up her pace, not wanting to lose sight of Cee in what no doubt was a maze of an interior.

She stepped into the debris-filled shell of what was once, it looked like, a metal factory. Molten lava pots still hung from the walls, vats long sealed off still had traces of solid metal permanently melded to their sides.

Laura spotted Cee, a small speck of her, off to the left down a hall, and quickly followed.

She moved carefully, stepping over years of junk that had been tossed around, trinkets left to rot from the workers who'd up and left the building without so much as a backward glance, over broken floorboards with only darkness below.

Up ahead, Cee stepped through a door, a light on the other side.

Laura strained her eyes to the crack in the door, trying to see what lay beyond it.

Closer she stepped, until she could peer inside, the dim glow just enough to illuminate a sliver of her face.

It was a room. And there were one, two, maybe three people inside. No one was talking or moving. They stood up, staring at something Laura couldn't see.

The sound of a large metal door opening and closing rang out through the factory, seeming to shake its walls.

From behind Laura, something echoed.

She spun around, but saw nothing. Only a crumbling hallway in an abandoned building, little patches of snow gliding in gently from the open roof above.

When she turned back to the room, an eye was looking at her.

Laura screamed as the door flung open, as a hand reached out from the light and pulled her in, tossing her to the ground.

She fell hard against the grated metal floor, cutting her hand. Laura sat up, clutching her palm, the blood seeping out.

"What the fuck?" she screamed, looking at the three women in the room, their eyes not on her, but on her hand. "Where's Cee?"

The women exchanged glances.

"Is this a test?" one of them asked.

"She left her for us."

"No."

"She must have."

None of the women moved. They stood over Laura, watching her, weighing their options.

Laura pushed herself along the floor. She pressed her back against a large, rusted metal door, the one she'd heard open and close, as the women each took a step toward her. They blocked the wooden door, and the only window in the room was spiked by its own broken pane—the only way out was wherever Cee had disappeared through.

Laura shot up and banged on the door with both hands, her own blood smearing against the rust. "Cee! Cee!"

But it was too late.

One of the women jumped on Laura, pulling her back, onto the ground. The two others grabbed her by the arms and dragged her up onto her knees, facing the door. Laura tried to get her hands free, she tried to wiggle away, to get her pepper spray, but they held her with firm grips. She could only watch as the woman before her, a woman with a pockmarked face, fished something out of her pocket.

She took a patient step toward Laura, darkness clouding her eyes. The closer she crept, the more Laura could see what she held in her hands: a rusty blade.

"Cee!" Laura cried again, but it fell upon deaf ears. Laura turned back to the pockmarked woman instead. "I'm trying to find my mom. Her picture's in my pocket. Maybe you've seen her?"

But the woman was hungry. She unhitched the blade and brought it to Laura's neck.

"This is my initiation," the pockmarked woman said, flashing a mouth of rotted teeth. "You're my way in."

"No, stop—" Laura pleaded, but the rest of her words slipped away as the woman dragged the rusted blade across her throat.

Laura had always assumed that her life would flash before her eyes in the moments leading up to her death. She'd thought that memories with Mary, good ones buried deep inside her, would surface, showing themselves for the first and last time. She'd thought that she'd be able to look back on her life and be proud of what she'd achieved, of what she'd accomplished.

But as the three women stepped away from Laura, as Laura brought her hand to her throat to close the spreading wound, as the smallest trickle of blood seeped out from in between Laura's fingers and into the drain below, she saw nothing.

Nothing but her trembling hand catching droplets of her own life, spilling out from her.

Laura collapsed onto her stomach, one hand out to catch her, one hand still clutching her wound. It felt deep. Wide. Like the woman had tried to sever her head from her body.

She tried to breathe.

She gasped for air.

Nothing seemed to be coming in.

The women approached her again, putting their hands under her to catch her falling blood. They brought their own hands to their mouths and licked their fingers, letting out satiated moans.

And then, the sound of a large metal door opening echoed throughout the room.

Laura craned her head up to see Cee staring down at her, dark, burning eyes with a fire igniting inside them.

Laura's head fell back to the floor, her cheek against the harsh metal, her gaze finding the drain beneath her. She watched, mesmerized, by the sight of her own blood circling into the pipe.

She felt hands around her neck, hands trying to flip her over, hands trying to rip her open even more.

And then the hands disappeared, and Laura heard what sounded like two raw eggs hitting the wall.

Laura rolled herself over, coughing and wheezing and feeling the blood pouring into her lungs.

The pockmarked woman stood between her and Cee. She dropped the knife onto the floor with a *cling*, her eyes full of fear, her eyes on Cee. Then she rushed past Cee, a feeble attempt to make it to the metal door, trying to open it, trying to force herself into the life she wanted.

But Cee wouldn't allow it.

Cee grabbed the pockmarked woman and threw her down onto the grate with a strength she didn't look like she possessed.

The woman begged and pleaded for her life, but Cee was deaf to it all, driven only by the rage that boiled up inside her.

The woman screamed as Cee put her boot against the woman's head, pressing down into the metal grate until the pressure became too much.

The woman's head split.

Without missing a beat, Cee scraped Laura off the floor and into her arms.

She threw open the door into the Underground, leaving the remains of the three women to drip into the drain below.

XI

Laura jolted up. For a second, she thought she was in her own home with the wilted walls and the way it stank of decay; in her own bed, with the threadbare sheets and thin comforter.

She wasn't home. She was in a metal box, tucked into a thin mattress that rested on the floor. Three of the walls were even more rusted than the large metal door in the waiting room, while the other was brick. The walls were covered in shelves, and each shelf had about a million different trinkets on it, trinkets that, in this light, looked to be nothing more than trash.

She looked for a window, but none existed, the only light bleeding in from the crack under the door and a dim glow from the loosely hanging bulb attached to a cord above. Against the far wall, near the corner, Laura noticed a protruding pipe, the hole of the pipe itself glistening in the low light with chunks of something stuck to it.

She was in the Underground.

Cee rested on the floor next to her, a blanket her only comfort against the metal grating. Laura eyed Cee as she dreamed, her short dark hair that framed her scarred face, even while she rested. And her scars, they ran around the perimeter of her face, but stopped near her ear, as though someone had cut at her skin, wanting to remove her face, then changed their mind.

Laura's hands found her way to her throat then.

She sprung out of bed, eyes scanning the shelves until she spotted an old hand-held mirror among the chaos.

Laura brought the mirror to her neck.

The wound was gone.

In its place was a fresh patch of skin.

It looked the same as her stomach. It had been mended by the same hand.

Laura ran her free fingers over the graft, feeling the slight bump where old skin met new.

How is this possible?

"You're up." Laura spun around to see Cee rising from her makeshift bed. "How are you feeling?"

Laura, with her hand still on her throat, glared at Cee, unsure if she should be terrified or grateful. The pieces slowly started falling into place in Laura's mind—the attack in the alleyway, and now, this. "You saved me. Twice."

Cee stood up, her dark eyes meeting Laura's; mouth looking for the right words to say.

Instead, Cee moved closer to Laura, bringing her hands to Laura's neck.

Laura shivered at Cee's cold touch, expelling a nervous breath into the air. She kept her eyes on Cee, allowing her to run her fingers across her neck, looking over her own work.

Cee's touch felt right to Laura. It felt familiar.

"I'm glad you're okay," Cee finally said, the weight of the words not lost on Laura as Cee's hand still lingered on her neck.

"How am I still alive?" Laura whispered back, a new heat rising inside of her, not of anger, but of desire.

"I fixed you," Cee looked up from Laura's neck, their faces only inches apart.

"Tell me how."

Laura could see the thoughts in Cee's eyes, the intensity, the pain behind them.

"It's something someone taught me a long time ago. A skill necessary for survival."

Cee's gaze fell from Laura's eyes to her lips, and Laura's followed suit.

Laura stood motionless, watching as Cee drew her face toward hers, breathing Cee in. Every fibre of her being screamed at her to stop, to pull away, to run out of the Underground and back to the outside world.

But Laura didn't want to.

In this moment, all she wanted was Cee.

An abrupt knock at the door caused them both to break away. Cee's icy hands fell from Laura's neck, leaving her to shiver at their memory.

Cee looked to the door, the shadow of the person outside stepping away, their job done.

"There's someone you should meet," Cee sighed.

Yellow lights casted their rusty hue over everything they passed as Laura followed Cee through the Underground—the metal floor, same as the waiting room, her boots clinking against it as they walked. And above, the ceiling, just as maze-like and winding as the corridors, lined with metal pipes whose former glory was lost to their flaking exteriors. The walls themselves not much different—more pipes still, bending over doorways, travelling under the grated flooring, and hissing and spitting at almost every turn. Most of the doors they passed were closed as they continued down the never-ending hallways, but Laura found one or two that were ajar. She snuck a look into those, seeing rooms with a similar layout to Cee's, some brick walls, some metal; metal flooring, and the same pipe against the corner, layered with uncleaned chunks of whatever spilled from it.

And the smell, the stench of metal and electricity, embedded itself into Laura's pores. She brought her sleeve to her mouth and nose in a poor attempt to filter out some of it, but it proved useless.

Given the sights and the smells, the sublevel abandoned factory was eerily quiet. The normal noises of an abandoned factory abounded—a quiet hum emanating from within the walls, something Laura assumed was from whatever they used to keep the electricity up and running.

What was missing was the sound of people.

They'd crossed no one, seen no one as she'd traipsed down a set of stairs, which opened up to a cavernous middle, like a large elevator shaft—a square area with staircases leading down every side, those sides leading to even more hallways with even more pipes.

The Underground seemed to go on forever.

And Mary was down here somewhere.

Laura kept her mouth shut as she followed Cee a few levels down, her gaze shifting from the mystery of their destination to the back of Cee's head. As Cee walked, her sweater shifted, a hint of the skin under her hairline coming into view—though Cee stood several inches taller than Laura, Laura could see a scar that seemed to go under her hair. A perfectly centred scar that traversed down her neck and disappeared into her sweater.

They continued on down a hallway, toward a heavy-looking set of double doors, just as rusted and metallic as everything else.

Cee stopped before the doors, hands at her sides. Laura stood next to her.

Cee turned to Laura. "You don't have to do this."

"Do what?"

Cee took a moment, making sure she said exactly what she meant. "Meet her. We could . . . "

Laura could sense Cee's hesitance, but Laura wasn't ready to give up yet, especially after how far she'd come, after how much she'd suffered. The answer to Mary's whereabouts was right behind the door that stood before them. She wasn't about to back away now.

"We could what?" Laura asked, but Cee swallowed her words. Laura turned back to the door. "I think we both know what I have to do."

Cee nodded, her head hanging low. "Let me do the talking," she said.

Then she reached out to the handles and pushed both doors open.

The stench was the first thing to strike Laura, an even more extreme assault on her senses than the rest of the Underground.

In this room, it stank of rot. Of decay. Of age.

It reminded Laura of the time one summer when a stray dog that roamed around her town had somehow gotten itself caught in the crawlspace underneath her home. She'd never been sure if it had been injured beforehand and had found a break in the lattice that separated ground and her home and couldn't get out, or if it deliberately gone there to die, but whatever had happened, that poor dog hadn't stood a chance.

It had decided to take its last breaths directly under her room.

And her room had never quite smelled the same after that.

This room—this chamber—she stood in now was double the size of her tiny house. Windowless as the rest, the calcium deposits seeped down the rusted amber walls with greens and blues and reds, as though they were in a cave system untouched by humankind for centuries.

Her gaze followed the weeping walls to the back of the room, to the old, massive boiler that had once kept the factory thriving in its prime.

Now, it hummed a low sound that filled the space like a chanting choir. Laura could see the faintest hint of fire in its belly. It spanned the width of the chamber, encapsulating the entire back wall. It was more imposing than anything and must've been quite the sight when it had been operational.

The floor itself was littered with trash. Years of it. The piles ebbed and flowed like angry waves crashing against a silent beach. Her eye caught several random things: stuffed animals, crumpled papers, broken needles, burned diaries, broken photo frames, things that once belong to others, now collected here, in piles.

At the centre of the room, just before the boiler, the trash had been cleared out in a path.

At the end of the path was a makeshift throne made up of metal shards and broken pieces of glass, all forged together to mimic the square shape of the boiler, as though this seat and the boiler were born of the same womb.

And on the throne of metal and glass, sat a woman.

The woman from the mural.

Mother.

She wore what looked like a robe, one long enough to cover her entire body and much of the chair itself. Only visible was her face and some of her neck, and even then, her long, raven-black hair covered most of it, hair that Laura thought looked similar to her own.

She was pale, unnaturally so. Her eyes were dark like Cee's, old eyes that didn't seem to match her young, flawless skin.

She was both monstruous and beautiful at the same time.

"Mother," Cee was suddenly in front of her, as though shielding Laura from Mother's gaze. "Thank you for—"

"I was told you know where my mom is," Laura interrupted, taking a step in front of Cee. She'd waited long enough. She needed answers now. "Do you?"

Laura could feel the woman's eyes on her, studying her. Laura kept her head up and her gaze on the woman's. She'd been stared down at enough in life to know when to look away and when not to. Not that she wanted to—like Cee, there was something about Mother that Laura wanted to explore more of. They were both intoxicating.

Mother stood and adjusted her cloak, her pale hands creeping out from the armholes. Her hands, like her eyes, didn't match the rest of her body, even under the many rings and bracelets that adorned them. They were old, wrinkled, veined. Mother quickly tucked them back inside the fabric. She seemed to float as she moved closer to Laura and Cee, her eyes never leaving Laura's.

The closer the woman got, the more intimidated Laura felt, like she should be shrinking down into the fetal position on the dirty ground. Mother was within inches of her face, looking her over from head to toe. She brought an old hand to Laura's cheek, gently brushing against her bruises.

"I have a picture . . . " Laura began, pulling an old photo of Mary from her pocket. She passed it to Mother, who didn't look.

"What happened to your face?" Mother asked, ignoring Laura's question. Her voice was like a whisper in a loud room, a gentle, feminine tone, like that of a patient teacher.

"I . . . was attacked."

Mother's hands found their way to Laura's throat, to the newly-patchworked lump. "And someone fixed you up quite nicely."

Mother then grabbed Laura's hands, hands even colder than Cee's, causing Laura to drop Mary's photo onto a pile below. Laura didn't notice—she was too enthralled by Mother.

Mother flipped Laura's hand over, her gaze resting on Laura's port wine birthmark.

"Beautiful," she said.

With one quick movement, Mother rushed her hands out of Laura's, causing something to cut against Laura's palm, reopening the wound she'd gotten from falling to the waiting room floor.

Laura pulled back immediately, wincing at the growing sting. She flipped her birthmarked hand over and saw blood beginning to spill from it.

"What the fuck?" Laura clutched her palm. She looked back at Cee, but Cee kept her eyes down.

Mother turned away. With her back turned to the women, she brought her own hand to her mouth, subtlety licking at her index finger.

"Mother . . . " Cee began.

"Mary is here," Mother said as she tucked her hands away and took a seat, eyes on Laura.

The room almost felt like it faded away as the realization of Mother's words hit Laura. "What? You're sure?"

"I never forget a face," said Mother.

A tension seemed to lift itself off of Laura's shoulders then, even though her rules— *Don't make eye contact.*

Trust no one.

Always be ready to defend yourself.

—screamed at her from inside.

"I'll bring you to her," Mother continued, "but you need to do something for me first."

Laura's heart raced in her chest. "Yes, anything."

Cee tensed beside her.

"Go with Cee tonight—"

"No," Cee suddenly burst out, interrupting Mother. "Please. That's not . . . "

Laura watched as Mother glared at Cee, her old hands with their sharp nails digging into her throne. Cee tried to hold her gaze, tried to continue speaking, but ultimately looked away.

"Go with Cee tonight," Mother continued, "and bring me an offering. Then we'll have a deal."

"Yes," Laura said. "Anything you want."

"Anything I want," Mother said, her low voice suddenly taking on some of Laura's inflections. "Go now. While the night belongs to you."

Laura nodded, forgetting all about everything that had happened to her up until that point—Mary was within her reach. She could have her mom back by the end of the night, then she'd drag the woman home and lock her in the basement, if that meant never having to come back to the city, to the Underground. This nightmare was almost over.

"Thank you," was all Laura could manage as her and Cee exited the room.

XII

Cee stormed out of the Underground, past the empty waiting room, cleaned by some of the many unseen souls who inhabited Mother's world, and out onto the snow-filled street beyond the factory.

"Cee, wait," Laura had called out after her the entire journey out. But Cee was seething. Mother had played her into a corner, another blow to her freedom. And Cee had been the idiot who'd led Laura to the Underground.

But seeing Laura on the ground as she had that first night, after she'd been attacked, the same feeling had struck her once more. There was something about Laura, something she couldn't shake. She needed to save her, to keep her alive. Laura was resilient, tenacious—she wouldn't let anyone stop her from doing what she wanted to do, a quality that Cee often wished she'd possessed. If she had it, maybe she wouldn't have gotten stuck in this life.

And leaving wasn't as simple as packing up your bags and heading out the door. Others had tried it, once they saw the Underground for what it really was, and those who'd been caught (sometimes by Cee's own hand) had been dealt with accordingly.

When you made an oath to Mother, to serve and protect her, you made it for always.

But Cee had been dreaming of escape for some time. Her plan, though not foolproof, would certainly buy her enough time to head east, to more largely populated cities, to where it was easier to stay lost, where it was easier for no one to find you, if you didn't want to be found.

And Laura would be Cee's ticket out.

Away from Mother, away from this life, or whatever it was. She could be free. She knew she could. But she wanted to be free with Laura.

She could feel the bond forming between them, a fire inside both their eyes that lit whenever their gazes met. Cee had saved Laura, after all. That first night, after her attack, as Cee went to work in the back alley, patching Laura's skin with remnants of Mother, with pieces made specifically for Cee to use on herself, she'd done something she hadn't done in some time—she took a taste of Laura's blood.

Cee was tired of Mother's leftovers, fed to her through the tube in her room. She'd often thought about the earlier days, how Cee would be able to eat straight from the source, but now that Mother's operation had grown, she kept it all for herself, only sharing the unwanted bits with those who lived to serve her.

And Mother knew whenever Cee would bring an offering back to the Underground, if Cee had taken the first bite or the first sip. Mother would never divulge that to the populace, but rather, behind closed doors, in her chamber, where Cee would face the brunt of Mother's wrath.

Ten lashings was the usual punishment. Ten lashings without the ability to patch the skin until a week later, when the hanging, rotting flesh had turned black, when the smell had seeped into Cee's very clothes, her skin and the fabric becoming one and the same.

And then Mother would patch her, using her own skin, tending to Cee like a real mother to her child with a scrape.

Cee had found it comforting, at first, to be given such love and affection, but now, now Cee saw it for what it really was: a distorted relationship between a kidnapper and their victim. And Cee was tired of hiding her scars underneath her clothes.

"Hang on," Laura's voice called out again.

Cee came to a stop in the middle of the road, the night hanging heavily over them.

"I told you to keep your mouth shut," Cee spat, catching Laura off guard. "Now look at the mess we're in."

"Excuse me," Laura spat right back, eyes as black as Cee's. "We wouldn't be in any mess if you hadn't brought me down there in the first place."

"I brought you down there to save your life. I brought you exactly where you wanted to go. And now . . . " Cee trailed off. *And now you have to kill someone*, she wanted to say.

"What?" Laura's voice was stained with frustration. "What, huh? I'm this close to finding my mom and getting the fuck out of this hell, and now you want to stop? It must be so easy for you, to just throw me away. You have no idea what I've done to get here. No idea. And I'm not stopping now. I'll do whatever it takes to get her back."

Cee bit her tongue. She wanted to tell Laura the whole of it—how Mother was always one step ahead; how, even if Laura did find Mary, Mother wasn't going to let either of them go. They needed to run. They needed to get as far away from this place as they could.

But as the women stared each other down in the stillness of the night, as the rage began to subside in both their eyes, Cee didn't have the heart. Laura had already been through so much. Who was Cee to cast her out once more, even if it meant saving her?

So she formed a new plan: find Mary, if she was still alive, and get the three of them out.

This was the only way.

"Are you sure you want to do this?" Cee asked Laura, even though she already knew the answer.

XIII

They wandered for hours, keeping to the shadows of every back alley, every back door, every forgotten road.

They passed by different people from different walks of life, but none were the right one for Mother, according to Cee.

Laura watched her with a curious eye, this tall, slender woman with her scars. Laura still wasn't sure on what their task was—*an offering*, Mother had said, leaving it at that. She could only surmise what that meant, and had been grappling with it since the words left Mother's mouth. But the more they walked, the more Laura knew—she would do whatever it took to get Mary back.

They rounded a corner, deep within the labyrinth of the city.

Suddenly, Cee stuck her arm out, stopping Laura in her tracks.

"What is it?" Laura whispered, eyes on Cee.

Cee glared down the alleyway, to the distant sounds of someone rummaging through a nearby dumpster.

Laura followed Cee's gaze and saw a down-and-out man going through the trash's contents. She looked back to Cee—a hardness has spread across her features.

Cee motioned at Laura to stay. Laura did as instructed, putting her hands into her pockets and looking back to the lights of the street in case someone happened to be walking by.

Cee approached the man with caution, her eyes never leaving his face. He finally looked up from his trash, eying her from underneath his wool hat.

"Hey," Cee said. "Are you okay?"

The man looked at her with a confused glance, but said nothing.

"It's just that it's really cold out tonight and you look like you could use some warming up. I know a place, if you want to go."

The man looked to the dumpster, then back to Cee, considering his options.

Laura watched them nervously from where she stood, the silence of the moment pulsating around her.

"I've heard stories," he began, "about people out here, about how you need to watch your back."

"I've heard those stories, too," Cee forced a smile. "Which is why you should come with us. We'll keep you safe."

The man eyed Cee, then Laura.

Slowly, he nodded.

"Great," Cee said. "Me and my friend will take you there."

Cee started toward Laura. The man took a few steps forward, then stopped.

The women turned back to him.

His face had changed.

"I've heard stories about *you*," he said, his eyes scanning Cee's face. "About how you steal people. How you take them to a place where you go in, but you don't come out."

Laura eyed Cee. Cee kept her cool. "That's ridiculous," she said, playing it off. "We're just going to warm spot to rest for the night. Nothing more. Now come on."

Cee reached a hand to the man, grabbing the crook of his sleeve. She pulled at him a little too hard, her impatience getting the better of her.

The man pulled away, retreating back toward the dumpster.

"No," he said then, "No, I won't go with you. No!"

The man began to scream. His cries echoed out into the silent night, bouncing off of every surface, every wall that surrounded them.

"Shut up!" Cee yelled back, over and over, but the man wouldn't stop.

Laura looked back to the street—no one had come, yet.

This man was going to ruin her one chance to save Mary.

She couldn't let that happen.

Laura rushed over to the man, pushing past Cee, hands coming out of her pockets.

Then, she hit him in the face with her pepper spray.

He keeled over at the agent hitting his skin. He screamed into the night, his shouts shifting from fear to pain.

Cee turned to Laura with a look of disappointment in her eyes.

The man stood up then and tried to run, but he ran straight onto a patch of ice.

He stumbled forward, smacking his head against a sharp corner of the dumpster, hard.

His body slid to the ground, face first into the snow, as blood began to pool around him.

Cee remained silent. Laura turned to her, seeing the hard lines shifting her features. Her face seemed to change in front of her. There was something terrifying in her eyes. Something primal.

"Cee?" Laura asked, but Cee was gone, consumed only by the blood before her. Laura pulled at Cee's arm, but it was like trying to move a stone.

Laura opened her mouth to call for her again, but Cee was already off, pushing Laura aside, bounding toward the body, climbing on top of him in a flash.

"Cee! Stop!"

She had turned the man's head farther than a head was meant to turn, and was sucking at the wound, lapping up the fresh blood.

Laura watched, unable to say anything or do anything to stop her. This was who Cee really was—a hunter. An animal.

Cee continued to suck until there was nothing left inside the man.

She stood up, a sense of calmness washing over her. She then saw Laura staring at her, and a shame seemed to spread into her eyes as she wiped away at the blood stains around her mouth.

But Laura didn't feel her shame. She didn't feel scared or threatened or anything that would make her want to run away.

Laura felt exhilarated.

Suddenly, Cee fell to her knees, clutching at her stomach in writhing pain.

"What's wrong?" Laura asked. "What's happening?"

"The blood . . . " she began before going onto all fours and vomiting all the blood and gore she'd just consumed out onto the snow.

"His blood . . . " she said again between laboured breaths, "it's tainted."

"Tainted with what?"

"Whatever he'd gotten into," Cee managed once more before purging again.

"What do you need? What can I do?"

"My . . . room . . . I need to . . . feed . . . "

"Let's go," Laura propped Cee up, throwing her arm over her.

The two moved through the night, Laura carrying the brunt of Cee through the snow, into the industrial area, and back into the hallways and mazes of the Underground.

Laura threw Cee's door open. Cee stumbled in, scrambling to

the bucket at the far end of the room, the one that caught the blood that Mother fed to her followers.

Cee dipped her hands into the container and brought a cupful to her mouth. She swallowed it whole, little streams of crimson trickling down the sides of her mouth.

But still, she vomited.

"This isn't . . . " Cee said in a shiver, " . . . I need fresh . . . yours."

Cee's eyes met Laura's.

"My blood?"

Cee nodded, the colour, of what little she had, completely drained from her face. "Knife . . . pocket . . . "

Cee was shivering now. Laura dug through her back pocket and pulled out a dull, blood-encrusted blade.

"Please . . . "

Laura held the blade in her hands. It looked heavy, but felt light to the touch. Laura brought the dull blade to her wounded palm.

She took a breath and reopened it, wincing at the sting.

Fresh blood dropped onto the grated ground.

Laura sat down, propping Cee's head in her lap. Then she brought her palm to Cee's mouth, and Cee began to drink.

It felt strange, Cee's cold lips on her hand, Cee's tongue poking at the gash, in a desperate search for more.

But as Cee fed, her cold hands gripped Laura's. And she couldn't shake the feeling of how right this all felt, even as strange as the situation was.

They could have a life down here, her and Cee and Mary. This was so much better than the house she lived in. She felt protected here. She felt safe.

Laura took her other hand and ran it through Cee's short hair, pushing it away from her face, tracing the scars on her skin as she fed from her.

Cee had fallen asleep in Laura's lap, and Laura didn't have the heart to move her.

Laura watched as her chest rose and fell as she dreamed. She looked around Cee's room with more time to observe, noticing all the little knickknacks and trinkets that lined her walls—shelf after shelf of random items, a baseball and a music box, a porcelain figure of a child in a snowsuit, and a half-empty pack of gum. It reminded Laura of Mother's chamber, with all the personal items strewn about.

Laura's eyes continued around Cee's room, tracing the old bricks on her one bricked wall. The mortar, once supposed to keep them together, now threatening to crumble apart.

But one brick, one brick looked out of place. Like the mortar had already been picked away.

Ever so carefully, Laura wedged herself out from under Cee's head, letting it rest against her thin pillow. Cee didn't so much as budge—she was out cold.

Laura then crept over to the one brick, quietly prying her fingertips in and around it, pulling at the stone until it slid out its hole and into Laura's hands.

The gaping hole beyond was dark, but Laura reached a hand into the darkness nonetheless. It was deep, going up to her elbow. Her fingers pushed and prodded at what felt like dust, until they finally touched something solid.

As quiet as a mouse, she pulled the something out, then moved closer to the door, to the crack of light spilling in from underneath.

It was a vintage box with some weight to it, well-worn and well-loved. Laura opened the box, revealing a collection of trinkets and jewelry—the more personal items that Cee didn't want to display.

She rummaged through its contents—half a carnival ticket, a football championship ring—then pulled out an old newspaper clipping.

Laura unfolded it. The paper was soft to the touch, like any sudden movement could render it to dust. The short article, dated February 15, 1952, was about a young girl who'd gone missing and who was presumed dead. No photo, not much more than the first initial of a name. The name itself lost to the torn part of the paper that no longer existed, one single letter all that remained—C.

Cee stirred then, and Laura quickly folded the paper and put it back into the box.

She was about to close the lid when the outside light caught something with a shine.

Laura dug through the items, pulling out the item.

A necklace.

She picked up the locket, letting it twirl in her fingers.

The light from under the door caught it as it spun, filling the room with a golden glow.

XIV

When Cee woke up, she was alone, though Laura's warmth still lingered inside of her.

Laura's blood had done exactly what it needed to do—revitalized her. It had flushed the remnants of the tainted man out, it had replenished her in a way that Mother's recycled blood couldn't do. She felt better than ever, and now, she was ready to tell Laura the truth of it all—about Mary, about Mother, about what the Underground really was.

About how they had to leave.

Cee stood up, still a little shaky, wandering over to her door. Her foot caught on something in the dark. She flipped on her light and saw her trinket box, open on the ground, for all prying eyes to see.

Cee frantically bent down, poring over each and every item.

They were all accounted for, except for one.

The golden necklace was gone.

And so was Laura.

Cee tore through the Underground. How could she have been so stupid, bringing Laura back to this place, especially after they'd failed in the simplest of tasks? How could she have been so moronic to deliver Laura straight to a *thing*—not a woman—who fed off people like Laura? She'd been so blinded by her own escape, by Laura, by a false sense of happiness, that she hadn't seen the truth of what was right in front of her—that Mother had her claws in everything.

And that Cee could never escape. At least, not while Mother was still alive.

Cee raced through the hallways, sprinted down the stairs, leaped for the rusted metal doors leading to Mother's chamber.

She threw them open, expecting to see Mother and Mother alone, with any sign of Laura long gone like anyone else who'd come to the Underground without being initiated.

But that wasn't the case.

Mother was on her throne, and there were two others inside with her.

One of them was a man, a new man, shaking and crying and on his knees, pleading for his life.

The other, the person holding a dull blade to the man's throat, was Laura.

"Laura, stop!" Cee called out, her voice echoing throughout the room.

Both Laura and Mother looked to Cee—Mother with anger in her old eyes, Laura with a glazed-over expression, her youthful glow all but faded away.

Cee sprinted toward Laura, reaching for her arm. "Stop, please, you don't have to do this."

Laura watched Cee, dead-eyed, the knife still at the sobbing man's throat.

"She can do what she pleases here," Mother interrupted. "Including the task that I sent you to do. Sweet Laura went to go finish the job herself. That's the kind of woman I want serving beside me. That's how you used to be. What happened?"

"What happened? What happened is that I wanted to live down here, with you, forever, but not like this. I'm sick of doing your dirty work. And for what? What have you given me except for pain?"

Mother jolted from her seat. "What have I given you?" the anger was seething in her voice. "I've given you everything."

"Hey!" Laura interrupted, her gaze focused solely on Mother. "You said if I delivered you an offering, you'd bring me to my mom. Well, here it is. Now show her to me."

Mother turned her attention to Laura, her voice softening. "Tell me, why do you fight so hard for someone who wouldn't do the same for you?"

Laura stared at Mother. Her eyes went down, thinking of what to say.

"If your mother loved you, truly loved you, would she have left you alone? Would she not have cared for you or nurtured you or told you not to come here to search for her?"

Laura's gaze fell from Mother's as a sob escaped her lips.

"Sweet child, don't cry," Mother said, slinking toward Laura. "I understand. I know that hopelessness inside of you. I felt it too, a long time ago. But I sooner realized that my true family was one of my own making, not the one I had been born into. Down here, we're family. No one will cast you out. No one will bat you aside. We choose who we love."

Laura fell into Mother's arms then, engulfed in her dark robe. Mother stroked her hair as the sobbing man quietly slipped past them both, to the locked double doors.

"Your mother doesn't love you," Mother whispered into Laura's ear. "You were only a burden to her. But to me, you're so much more. I see the potential in you, Laura. I see a daughter to call my own."

Laura stepped out of their embrace, staring up at Mother with the stars in her eyes. Cee could tell—Laura was gone, like so many of the others, like she had once been, stolen by the warm words and false promises.

Mother brought a wrinkled hand over Laura's cheek, brushing away her tears.

Still, Cee had to try.

"Laura, let's go—" Cee reached out for Laura, but Laura pulled away, not even casting a glance toward her.

And that's when Cee saw it—the golden necklace. It was hanging around Laura's neck, dangling near her heart.

"My necklace . . . " Cee trailed off.

"You mean my mom's necklace," Laura burst out, finally turning to Cee. "You stole this from her."

"No . . . " Cee began. "I . . . I didn't know her. I just . . . collect things. I found that necklace."

"Bullshit," Laura spat at Cee. "I know she's down here. I know what you did to her. Nancy told me to be careful around you, and I didn't listen. I should've."

"No, Laura . . . " Cee reached out for Laura again, but this time, Mother was there. She extended her hand quicker than Cee had time to react. The nail of her index finger struck Cee square across her jaw, slicing her open. Another future scar to add to her face.

Cee fell to the ground, instinctively bringing a hand to the gash. Only a black liquid spilled out, and only a small amount.

Cee turned back to Laura and Mother, watching as the two nodded in understanding, a tender moment unfolding between them.

Mother smirked. "Sweet girl, you've brought this man before me, but that is not the offering I need. What I need is his blood."

Laura exhaled a breath, then turned her eyes to the ground in front of her. Resting just below was the photo of Mary that she'd dropped the night before, hardly noticeable in the sea of trash.

Behind Laura, the man clawed and banged and rapped against the doors, but they were locked.

There was no way out.

Time slowed then.

Cee could feel the air leave the room like a vacuum had sucked all of it out. She felt herself move in slow-motion, her legs pushing her body off the ground, slowly propelling the rest of her forward, toward Laura as she marched toward the man, the knife in her hand.

But even as she screamed at Laura to stop, even as she sprinted toward her, she knew it was too late.

Laura came up behind the distracted man, and, without so much as a flinch, brought the blade across his neck.

Laura let the man's body fall to the ground, his blood spraying into the grated metal floor, mixing in with the blood of all the others in the pipeway. Blood that would be distributed to Mother's followers through the flaps in their rooms. The blood of their daily meals.

The double rusted doors opened then, and in stepped a handful of others, the women Cee had recruited, the ones Cee had made. Mother's guards. Her sentries.

Two tended to the man's body, while two others came up behind Cee and grabbed her by the arms.

Cee screamed out into the room, her cries echoing across the metal walls, into the pipes below, into the small fire of the boiler.

The two dragged her back, back into the hallway, away from Laura. She thrashed and pulled and kicked, but they overpowered her.

Laura kept her back to Cee the entire time, even after the doors closed and the room was still once more.

She turned to Mother, leaving the photo of her mom where it lay.

"I'd like to see Mary," Laura said, the emotion gone from her voice.

XV

Laura followed Mother down to the bottom-most level of the Underground, slightly shaking from what she'd done. She'd felt the man's life slip away from under her fingertips. She'd felt his lifeforce spill from the gash of her making, out into the world, ending his very existence.

And she had no regrets.

Except maybe for Cee, and the blind trust that she'd put in her.

But all she wanted to do now was see Mary and end this journey.

Laura watched as Mother walked ahead of her, flanked by her followers, women with pale, gaunt faces, women in unwashed clothes, the fabric stained with once-red droplets now turned brown. Mother walked like a woman with multiple hip surgeries, like a woman in need of a walker. Still, the tall figure trudged on, her shoes clicking against the metal flooring, and her loyal subjects seeing to her every move.

"When I first saw Mary," Mother said, "I thought she had once been a beautiful woman. I could see the remnants of what used to be under her tired skin."

They stopped in front of another set of rusted metal doors down a long hallway.

"She wanted a way out. She told me about you, that she wanted to leave you behind to give you a better life. A selfless act, I thought, likely the only one she's ever done. But here you are, out looking for the woman who wanted to give you up in exchange for all of this."

"Where is she?"

"Beyond these doors," Mother smiled, the skin around her lips folding in a strange way that made it seem like that part of her face was not her own. "Mary, though, there was something in her blood, something that told me that I should meet you, that you would be just as special as her, maybe even more. And when I tasted you, I knew I was right."

Laura looked at her hand, the cut still throbbing, the wound still open. "What do I taste like?"

"Youth," replied Mother. "It runs through you, through your blood, through your skin. It was in Mary, a hint of it, but there's more in you."

"And what about my wounds that Cee healed? How is that even possible?"

"Let me show you."

The doors opened into another metal room, this one larger than Cee's but smaller than Mother's chamber. Pipes ran in and out through the ceiling, the floor, the walls. And at its centre, sat a crudely made metal tub, deep and filled to the brim with a thick liquid that looked black in the amber light.

Mother moved toward it, her followers at her side as she did. Laura hesitantly followed, eying every inch of the space.

"What is this room?"

The workers set up a nearby table with a flurry of things that Laura couldn't see.

"It's a room of transformation."

Mother stood next to the tub, bending slightly to run a hand into the warm liquid. Her old eyes closed as the warmth travelled up her body. Then, she turned to Laura.

Laura watched in pure terror and fascination as Mother removed her robe.

The mural flashed back into Laura's mind—jagged lines cut across her skin like the Frankensteined faces of Laura's assaulters, her body a tapestry of colours. Her hands and her feet failed to match the rest of her—they appeared to be of the same skin, roughly cut around the edges, like a pair of socks and mittens.

Below her, the sea of pained faces—the servant women who helped her disrobe, who looked over her patchworked skin with love and care. The women she'd promised salvation to. The damned.

The skin on her face, it stopped below her collarbones, another jagged line adding to the fray, like someone had taken a pair of scissors and clumsily snipped away at the skin. The edges had blackened, the rot and decay seeping up the neck, threatening to encroach on the rest of the face in the coming days.

Mother was wearing a mask.

A mask made of someone else's face.

"Your hand," Mother commanded, holding out her own to Laura.

Laura, in a trance-like state, did as she was told. She placed her wounded palm up into Mother's, her touch beyond freezing.

With her free hand, Mother extended her index finger and cut at the seams near her belly, separating the two folds to reveal her true skin—greyish and rough, devoid of all warmth or colour, like old paint peeling off a wall. And from that skin, she cut a small rectangle and tore it from herself, placing it on Laura's wound, sealing it shut.

Laura felt a rush of cold run through her body as skin latched onto skin, watching in awe as the patch did all the work.

She examined her hand.

She was as good as new. The only hint that something was off on her palm were the mismatched colours.

Laura looked to the others around her and saw them weeping. They lowered their heads in praise of their master. Mother released Laura from her grip, then motioned her back.

Laura took a few steps behind her, closer to the table, to watch as the next phase of transformation began.

While the workers busied themselves by sewing Mother's flaps together, another one passed her a mirror. She gazed at her reflection, running her blood-soaked hands over her skin, stopping at the rotting edges.

"While this is a room of transformation, there's still one thing I've yet to master," she said, handing the mirror back to her followers.

"What's that?" Laura asked.

Mother brought her hands behind her, at the nape of her neck, digging her nails under the black, rotting flesh of her face. Then, she pulled, ripping the skin off of her own, pulling it off of her own face; the scalp—belonging to someone else—stayed behind. She dropped her mask to the floor.

Her true face was old, withered, and unlike anything Laura had ever seen. Her eyes looked human, but old. She had no nose, only a handful of small vertical slits, which led down to her lips, the skin coming together in bunches and folds as though she hadn't had a sip of water in centuries.

She was both beautiful and obscene.

Mother then ripped the scalp off of her head and passed it to one of her loyals. The woman carried it past Laura, to the table behind her.

The hair was raven-black and full, much like her own.

Much like Mary's.

Laura stepped back even more, hands behind her grasping for something solid, something real to hold onto.

Her reality was slipping away.

Everything was slipping away.

"Cee has been by my side for a very long time," Mother said unprompted, as she stepped into the tub, the liquid, clearly crimson, stopping just below her chin, the steam rising into the air. "I always feared the day would come when she would choose to leave me."

Mother turned her head, old eyes falling upon Laura, who bumped into the table, knocking some of the items out of place with a *clink*.

"She means much to me," Mother went on. "And I'm not ready to let her go."

Laura turned to the table. Knives, needles, and other things Laura had only seen on medical shows glistened in the room's orange light.

This place, she'd been blinded by it all.

By the glamour, by the false promises.

She'd broken all her own rules.

Don't make eye contact.

Trust no one.

And always be ready to defend yourself.

Laura grabbed one of the scalpels and held it out in front of her as the worker bees moved in.

"What are you?" Laura managed to whisper.

"I am God," Mother replied.

XVI

Cee paced around in her room. She hit at her door, ramming it as hard as she could. She screamed and yelled and kicked, but nothing worked.

She was locked in. She was trapped. Trapped in her own hell, in a cell of her own making. Trapped in a life she had asked for.

Laura wouldn't last a minute down in the Underground, not now that Mother had her hooks in her. It was only a matter of time before Laura became one of the faithful, working in processing or stitching, or worse, becoming part of their evening meal.

Suddenly, Cee's door unlocked, flinging open.

In stepped Laura, wide-eyed and frantic, bloodied and a little worse for wear.

But alive. Laura was alive.

She ran to Cee, throwing her arms around her.

"I'm sorry, I'm so sorry," Laura cried into Cee's shoulder, her voice shaky and muffled.

Cee held her close, breathing her in. Laura's sweet scent greeted her, hints of metals underneath it.

"What happened? How did you get away?" Cee pulled back.

"I was playing along," Laura said. "I told Mother exactly what she wanted to hear. Then, when I was shown to my own room, I came to find you. Now let's go. Let's get out of here before she finds out what we're up to."

"What about your mom?"

"She's . . . dead," Laura stammered, looking away from Cee. "Let's go."

Laura pulled at Cee's hand, and Cee started to move, but stopped herself.

For once in her life, she didn't give in to her impulses. Instead, she took a second to think.

If they up and left now, they'd be hunted. Mother was brash and unforgiving. She wouldn't simply let anyone walk away from her. She would stop at nothing until she got Cee back.

If they left now, they'd be on the run for as long as Mother was alive.

The creature was old, hundreds of years by Cee's guess. Who knew how much longer she had to live.

"Wait a second," Cee said. Laura spun around, the shadows heavy around her eyes. "We can't. I can't."

"What do you mean? Of course you can. Weren't you the one who wanted to go? Here's our chance. Let's take it."

"No, she'll find us, no matter where we go. She'll find us."

Laura sighed. "So what do you propose we do then?"

"We need to kill Mother."

XVII

Cee led the way, sneaking past the closed doors of the others, past those who wandered the halls. Night was when they were busiest, when those who'd been promised a safe life were constantly put to work.

Laura followed behind as they took quick steps down to the bottom-most level of the Underground, to where Laura had last seen Mother—in her room of transformation.

Cee and Laura peeked from around the corner of the doors leading to the room. The doors were unguarded.

"She's in there," Laura said, sprinting forward.

"Wait . . . " Cee called out, but it was too late. Laura was at the doors, turning their knobs.

Mother had her guards with her at all times, either in the room or standing outside it.

There had to be more inside.

Cee watched as Laura disappeared into the room.

"Laura!" she called out, chasing after her.

But inside, there were no guards. No sentries. No one ready to put their life on the line for this woman, this *thing*.

There was only Mother, soaking in her tub, the only visible part of her body her masked face.

Something's not right.

She was deep into the transformation process, a process that Cee had overseen many times. The body suit that she wore lasted longer, so much as she soaked it every so often, as she did now. And when one piece began to rot, they were quick to replace it with a new patch of skin from a fresh donor, often pieces of themselves, often those who didn't make it past initiation. The body suit acted as a safeguard against her natural skin, the one she gave up in return to her most loyal when they needed mending.

But Mother's skin never sat right on someone other than herself, so the women, like Cee, were left with uneven faces, with noticeable patches. They wore them as badges of honour. At least, Cee had. Once.

And Mother's masks, perfectly carved from the faces that Mother liked the most, they never lasted more than a year, even with a soak. They were eight months into this face, that Mother wore now in the tub, taken from a woman Cee had found sleeping in a bus shack one night. It'd been easy to persuade her to the Underground; she'd been too trusting.

Cee looked around the empty room, at Mother, deep in transformation now, asleep to the world until the ritual was complete.

Laura took a step next to Mother, looking her masked face over with care. Then, she turned to Cee, darkness in her eyes.

"You need to do it," she said, her voice cold. "You need to end this."

Cee stared at Laura, then at Mother. She knew that she had to. She knew that if she didn't, she'd never be safe. She'd never be free.

But Mother had given her so much. She'd seen Cee for who she really was all those years ago. Mother had given her something that no one else could've—life.

And Cee had tried to give Mother her own face, as a gift, as a thank you for giving her so much, but she hadn't been able to go through with it. She'd made the cuts, using her new finger, the one with the sharpened nail taken directly from Mother's own hand, but she hadn't finished.

She hadn't been able to do it.

"I don't know if I—"

Mother's eyes snapped open then. They darted to Laura, standing just within arms' reach.

Mother sprang up, her body stained red, and grabbed Laura, pulling her into the tub with a muffled scream.

Laura screamed back, fighting against Mother's grip.

The two women struggled, with Mother getting the upper hand, pushing Laura's head under the liquid, slowly drowning her.

But Cee, Cee was fast.

In an instant, she was at the tub, her hand at Mother's neck, her sharpened nail ready to drag across Mother's true skin.

Mother looked up at Cee at that moment, deep, dark eyes with a pleading glare in them. A muffled, muted scream came from her mouth.

But Cee had already started her finger across the flesh.

And in a moment, as Cee noticed a hint of a youthful glow in Mother's eyes, it was over.

Mother slumped into the tub, clutching at her neck.

Cee raced over and pulled Laura out. Covered in the black liquid, Laura inhaled deeply, letting the air come back into her lungs. She clutched at Cee as Cee helped her out, their grips still tightly woven around one another, Cee brushing the liquid from her face.

Cee turned and watched as Mother's eyes went dark, the light extinguishing from them, her masked face slipping into the darkened waters.

XVIII

Cee and a bloodied Laura crossed the threshold of the abandoned factory hand in hand, stepping out onto the snow-covered street.

They moved to the middle of the road and turned back to the factory.

Slowly, fire rose from the ruins, with everyone and everything down below having met their fate:

The others, who'd only wanted a safe life, a happy life, those who were content to serve their master until their demise.

The throne room, all of Mother's trinkets igniting the flames even more, the glass melting, the metal burning into itself.

Cee's room, all of her belongings going up in smoke, a true trial by fire. She would forget her past and only look toward her future now. A future that seemed brighter than ever, now with Mother gone.

And the last to burn, at the bottom-most level, the processing room, where all the skins burned, skins passed around for years, all genders, and all ethnicities.

Mary's skin burned.

So did Nancy's.

As did all the other random bits left behind, bits with imperfections, bits that Mother wanted to keep for herself in her private collection.

Like a patch with a port wine stain birthmark, the colour of strawberries.

Cee and Laura watched the flames consume it all, her whole life turning to ash before her eyes.

But she knew what lay beyond was better.

As long as she had Laura.

Laura turned to Cee then, sensing the power of the moment.

"You and me," Laura smiled.

Cee broke her gaze from the destruction. "You and me," Cee smiled back.

Laura's wrinkled hand gripped Cee's a little tighter as the reflection of the fire danced in her tired, old eyes.

ACID BATH

SOFIA AJRAM

I

"**FIRST TIME?**" Priya asks.

The guy's going matcha-green staring at the needle drawing up her blood like it's a hand grenade. He tells us he's an army sergeant. What a man like that's doing at a clinical drug trial is beyond me; guess he can handle a good bullet but not a little prick? Priya gives me that look, the vampiric one that says *bingo! We've found our guy,* 'cause she delights in fucking with first time piggies and these things have their ups and downs—you have to get your jollies where you can—so I launch right into the spiel.

"They ever tell you about the theralizumab drug trial?" I ask.

His gaze flicks between Priya and me. He shakes his head.

"Of course, they wouldn't." Priya flashes her teeth at him; grim smile. "It happened in '06, an in-human study designed for leukemia or whatever. They supposedly administered a dose five-hundred times lower than the safe dose in monkeys, but all of the volunteers—the non-placebo ones, anyway—ended up in the hospital for multiple organ failure."

"One guy straight up looked like the fucking Elephant Man," I say. *Tsk, tsk.*

Priya nods. "Yeah, he was a good looking guy before that. TX406 was way worse, though."

"Oh, fuck—" my eyes wide now, for dramatic effect. "Remember that? Injected the group, four days later and BOOM! One guy's dick *literally* fell off. Full-on detachable penis."

"And then there's the Van Gogh . . . "

"Yeah, yeah." Solemn nod. "The Van Gogh. That's the one where they sever your ear and stitch it back on for 5 g's."

When the army sergeant faints, we all get a laugh. Vasovagal syncope, Priya says when he rises, dejected and rejected from the trial. It happens to the best of us. Better luck next time. One could always try the fertility clinics or do sleep studies. Those aren't so bad if you're down with the pay cut and competition.

Me, Priya, and eight more make up ten in the waiting room; meat-puppets spawning like fulgurating spores. From straight edge weenies to neo-hippies, all walks of life show up here eventually. Hard to tell how many are involved in the drug study since they stagger the intakes. This one's been inundated with applicants because the stats on paper look good; proper compensation for outpatient research is such a rare drop I've never seen such a myriad of faces, this little ant-line of potential subjects walking to the intake room like peons in a strategy game, over and over, so many times that I can barely remember who's a patient or a nurse anymore. This one guy sitting next to the door, shaking like a shitting dog, told us he was in here to put food on the table for his kid. When the nurse called his name, "Gilbert McNutt," to the intake office, Priya and I set off cackling like crazed hyenas and spent the rest of the hour churning up name stupidities like Bart Simpson.

For we few who make it through, there's the blood draw, the EKG, the battery of questions, some tiresome, others flat out stupid. An inane game of Never Have I Ever with a forty-one paged stack of paper. *Describe your sleep habits. Describe your eating habits. Do you partake in recreational drug use? Do you smoke; drink? Have you ever considered harming yourself? Do you look at your own shit before you flush?* Yep, and I kiss it goodbye, too. Tearing down the list checking *Nope, nope, nope.* Answer in a range that's normal. Who's gonna know you smoked catnip at four o'clock in the morning, already high on amphetamines once? That shit's not going to show up on a piss test.

My favourite is: *How long has it been since you last did a study?* Because everybody default lies on that one. There's no universal database between these clinics, so everyone says, *oh, around eight months ago, was it? The last one I did was the last time I was here!* When, very typically, just a week ago you'd've been at some other study's cafeteria cashing in a meal ticket. Most recruiters, at least as far as I can tell from having done this shit for about two years now, know people are lying about that. The only reason they turn people away is because they don't want to enlist folks who freak or flake out. Urine tests don't check for drugs or caffeine in your system; they honest to god just take your word for it. If you do back-to-back—hell, even overlapping trials—it's fair game. That's the legalese beauty of private pharmaco, baby: everything is proprietary. Clinics can't get eyes on other recruiters' participant lists. So long as you're clean during the intake questionnaire and don't make a fuss or pass out when they put a catheter in your vein, they look the other way, and we look the other way, and we shake hands and make good on the itchy palms.

Sometimes I wonder if the doctors get off on that shit. When they shove a finger up your ass under the guise of a prostate exam on a trial that has absolutely nothing to do with your prostate, like giving a foot x-ray to a brain cancer patient. In college I had to do an elective course-load and one of the classes was Sexology, 'cause that sounded fun, and the first mandatory essay was writing about our entire sexual history; all of it, like from the first time you were two years old and ground one out against the bedpost, to your last dick appointment. I was twenty-one, and I did it—honestly, too. I really wonder what that old bitch did with all those stacks of student papers describing the first time they knew they had a foot fetish. That's kind of fucked up. Maybe the trial's the same, and these doctors have a whole spank bank of BTS footage of rectal exams.

Anyway, back to the matter at hand; two verbal interviews (hello, gender survey, my old friend), the attachment of an actigraph, urine test, and a finger up my ass later and I am approved for the trial, assessed by the team as "sufficiently psychologically robust" enough to participate in the group and research.

We get dispatched with a little paper list of expected side effects— headaches and constipation and all that noise. It's nice out. Summers in Montreal are warm, and I can feel Priya's hot breath on my skin when we sit at a public bench not far from the clinic and open our findings. Two kids with Halloween candy, each boasting the bigger find. Horse pills, the shit they gave us, and we gotta take three a day, and twice a week take it with a hypodermic. Trypanophobes need not apply.

I crack open one of the horse pills and pop my finger into the power, enrobe it with my lips. And—aw, fuck me. Of course, it's cornstarch. There's not a trace of the bitter lacing of actual medication. Priya is giving me a coy smile, sucking at a finger like a ring pop, so I know that bitch has got the real stuff.

"I'll trade ya," I say, and her smile grows large. She looks down at her phone and shoots off a text to her girlfriend, Nia.

You'd think you'd strike out if you are the placebo in the control group, but not so! Sometimes, the whole point *is* to take the drug; free amphetamines or antidepressants, the newest shit on the market. In many cases, you can walk away with thousands of dollars worth of free birth control or mood stabilizers; a six-month supply in double-bind studies of the brand name good-shit so long as you call in to your doctor every so often and rattle off a list of side effects.

Priya says she's going to use her payout to cover her tuition to this highly coveted, just-as-exclusive summer filmmaking workshop. Helix, it's called. Anybody who is anybody knows about this place. Damage is $4,800. USD. My eyes nearly bugged out of my fucking head when she said that, and I felt like she'd clocked me when she shared she got accepted. It's not that I don't think she can do it, it's just that the admittance rates on that place have got to rival Harvard's and she's just so *new* to it all. It's rare to see that sort of meteoric rise, and it floods me with acid jealousy the way she can just conjure up on a dime the perfect espousal of story and shots. It's hard to keep loving someone when their shadow overtakes you like a lunar eclipse.

In my case it doesn't matter. Money is not, and has never been, the draw. What gets me is curiosity. Couple weeks ago, Priya and I were shooting the breeze about this thing or that with some folks who knew nothing about piggy life when I thought about how making a short film about it would be cool—some sort of body horror clinical trial with symptoms of hanahaki disease, a fictional illness where someone will cough up flower petals, and then I found this clinical trial.

So the money's good and all, and I have enough from my parents to get me through the next couple years; their springy, comfortable net to catch me if I ever have any issues, but truthfully, what I want is the experience. Maybe that sounds stupid, but people thrill-seek in much dumber ways, diving out of airplanes and condomless fucking. This is a controlled kind of fuckery, one that will make good film fodder, and I'm certainly not the first. Scroll through that definitive list of *Old White Guy Books* filled with Acid Heroes literally all crypto bros own to tout that they have their soft, intellectual side, and you'll trip upon a medley of "man's man" authors who see themselves as outsiders for seeking the most violent and transgressive thrills over and over again in the name of art and literature.

I'd published one short film to mild Twitter success, and now I wanted more, looking for experiences to make it real. I do this with all things, from exotic dancing to subway busking. It makes for good stories at parties and is a magician's hat of endless and low-stakes resources to sieve through when screenwriting. You know what they say: write what you know, right?

Priya's a filmmaker, too. Sort of. In a lot of ways, we're cut from the same cloth, two Scorpios, roiling in emotion.

We met at a psych ward, barefoot, after I crawled onto the subway tracks (bad breakup + apathetic voice at the other end of a suicide hotline). Have you ever stayed at a psych ward? It's just like a fucking movie; the doors don't lock and the chairs rock so they're anti-tip and you get the good grippy socks. The ones up here in Canada you're not allowed to have your phone, all you've got is the shit DVD selection from god knows what era and food that rivals F-tier guinea pigging clinics. So really, when you're there, you make the most of it and get your jollies antagonizing the staff or exchange traumas in a blood-brotherly way with some other teen girl recovering from a fentanyl addiction. Priya would intentionally clog the toilet to piss off the head nurse and then go off skipping down the hall singing "Soeur Sourire" (*Domenique-nique-nique, S'en allait tout simplement! Routier, pauvre et chantant!*), clicking her heels. We licked each other's wounds. I liked her large, soulful eyes. The tenderness and strength there. Like a Botticelli painting. She made me feel normal and safe and loved, and when she left, she wrote her @ on my arm.

Maybe that was an experiment in experiences, too. Who's to say? Looking back, I'm glad I did it, glad I got to see what the inside of one of those places looks like. Like all these things, it's an experiment in loss of control, one you just have to endure, or tap out of. I can't remember why Priya was there, but she later wrote about it; put together a zine, *Survival Tips for Psych Wards*, that was a big hit at Expozine, tucked away in a church basement on St-Denis. Gained a lot of followers doing that, four or five thousand, so she kept going; zines on grief, surviving Mercury Retrograde, and the like, then moving to video format; low-budget sparsely edited digicam TikTok clips where poetics met life advice, like a big sister in an arthouse flick.

As far as I know, she isn't writing about this, though. This one is mine. Gonna make a short film and submit it, maybe to Toronto After Dark, maybe Small Gauge Trauma, the bigger, the better.

Which is why I want the real deal, the full monty. Some of these trials have ramp-up placebo, hard to tell which is first, but it defeats the whole purpose if I don't experience it myself. What am I gonna do, "interview" Priya? Bribe her doc for a peek? Fuck no.

I dig through my bag to find whatever errant trinkets may lie within that I can trade for Priya's pills, like someone rifling through their drawers for a reciprocatory holiday gift. In a side pocket, I grab a load of stickers I'd nicked at some store that sold Funko Pops. I hold up a handful.

"What if I sweeten the deal with a sick holographic Junji Ito sticker?"

Priya lowers her chin and lends me a smile. "You wait your turn, young man."

She knows how to make me feel good. My soul sings with the pronouns.

Still, I dig my hand through my bag to try and find something else that might appease her, a libation for the gods, 'cause I think I have a rose and terpenes baby vape hanging out at the bottom of my bag somewhere, and heaven knows Priya loves rose, she smells like a garden; but all I find at the bottom of my bag is a hole, the width of a finger; just big enough for pills (and a rose and terpenes baby vape pen) to pass through.

I twiddle my finger out the other end.

Priya looks down and makes a face.

The sun beams down on us, like a winking eye, bench beneath us hot as a highway blacktop.

"Wanna get out of here?"

"Priya, you precious diamond, you read my mind."

On the way home, we pop into an army surplus store. The place is filled with survival tools and tactical gear and Magnum combat boots, and guns if one were so inclined; all sorts of tchotchkes for doomsday types, soft reggae on the radio. There are some guys at the back dicking around with the gas masks and when one of them rubs the inside of it across his taint and tries to chase the other one around to put it over his head, Priya looks at me and simply says *cringe* in the most blistering way only women can, the offhanded cruelty of power by proxy of beauty.

I'm in there trying a different style. Something more overtly masc, though on my frame it's hard to pull off. I have this kind of spindly undeveloped thing going, so I glaze around in some Quasi-Boyhood. People who are close to me know the pronouns I like, and in the privacy of my room I shade my jaw with ochre pigment, wear the briefs and the binder, but on intake questionnaires I still tick off the Female box. Part of it is because I'm so used to the attention overt femininity gives to me. I know how to be a girl. I know how to be a girl *real fucking good.* I wonder what Priya thinks of me, unable to firmly step into any identity, living with my feet planted on both sides of seemingly everything: bi-racial, bi-sexual, non-binary, class-and-gender-ambiguity. There comes privilege with that. Maybe that's what I'm scared to give up, why I only take risks in controlled scenarios, like the clinical trial. Maybe, maybe, maybe. One could twirl around like a topper 'til it makes your head spin with all these maybes. I find comfort in maybe; between decision and choice. Having every door remain slightly cracked has a drug-like appeal.

I pull on a new backpack, way-too-big, but that army green I like. Priya says it looks cute, so I buy it. She steals a butterfly knife and some stickers from the front desk. Priya has scissors explicitly for shoplifting. Snip, snip. She doesn't even need my Junji Ito collection. She has a baseball card collection all her own.

Serves 'em right, she says on our way home. I know how she hates those Velcro patches and decals, not the ones who flaunt support for the armed forces, but the ones at the crossroads of stupid and conservative, *Thought my truck was dirty 'til I met your girlfriend,* and *This place is protected by a Pitbull with AIDS.* As dumb as they come.

II

Back home. Priya sighing into a kiss, stretching flat onto Nia's chest like a house cat; me in an immediate dive for the fridge and the depressing leftovers of—when the fuck did Nia make this vegan chilli?—no matter, have an iron stomach, and plonking myself down at the scratched-up leather La-Z-Boy by Nia's coffee table so I can see.

"This shit feels fucking *good*," Priya purrs. Nia asks if she means her tiddies as a pillow and Priya nuzzles into them and lets out a little *"mmm"*, and: "Yeah, but also whatever this shit is. I'm like—buzzed."

"What kind of drug is it?" Nia looks at me.

"Dunno." Shovelling chili into my mouth, chewing with the tip of the fork against my chin in simulacrum of thoughtful contemplation. "Antipsychotic or BPD thing, I think. Like, Thorazine or something, but more intense." She nods. This probably means more to her than me.

Feet propped up and watching her laptop screen, ghost-hunting shows or whatnot, that's her rerun guilty pleasure, and the incessant, prattling *ping!* of notifications signalling badges on all three of our cellphones.

"For fuck's sake," I hiss. Drop the plastic chili container into my lap and snatching my cell—family group chat popping off; pictures of babies and blue seas, my sister in Turks and Caicos with her kids—the group page for clinical trials, too, going apeshit, and I'm starting to get a stomachache, so I write that down. Jot down some notes in my phone, rattling off some symptoms. Totally inane, uninspired, and I sit up a little straighter when Priya suggests we take shrooms. I can work with that; stretch it into a narrative. All the best writers use drugs for inspo. Already I'm loosening my grip on the idea of centering this drug trial short film around myself—maybe I can make a movie and have it be about Priya. Or, it doesn't have to be *about* Priya, it can just be shots of Priya. Her and I on shrooms, I could fit that in with the hanahaki flower story somehow, and then assemble a narrative in post. I ask Priya if I can set up my phone in her bedroom under the pretense of recording some diary footage of us, and she agrees. Nia's only down for a baby dose, so Priya and I agree to move into her room once the visuals hit.

We talk for a bit and then take two and a half grams of golden teacher each around 1:00 p.m. or so; Nia taking half a gram and pairing it with edibles. Priya and I keep chatting about different things—lighthearted subjects, and then Priya says her "blood feels bubbly" after standing up to go to the bathroom. I'm not feeling anything yet.

We move to her bedroom; Nia stays in the living room watching ghost hunters on the couch.

Priya's bedspread is big, white, soft. I put my bag in the corner. The room is very humid, almost muggy; that dead mid-summer season that drains your energy like a black hole, makes you feel like you exist only within the singularity. There are two small side tables on either side of the bed, some framed photos of Nia on the wall, and on the opposite wall a photo of a saint slaying a dragon and a small shelf of stuffed animals.

We lie down on the bed lengthwise and start chatting, talking about books. She tells me about *Moby Dick*, that it's surprisingly funny and a little fruity. We're looking at the curtains; pink on the outside, white inside, as they gently billow in the breeze. Priya asks me if I can see the pattern in the blinds—looking closely, I don't think so, all that I tell her is that I can see the fibres that make the fabric—the weave of it, from afar. That's the best way I can explain it. It makes a shifting knit. She agrees: yes, a little, but for her it's rainbow-patterned.

We stare at the curtain for at least half an hour. Laughing, elated, the entire time. The curtain is so fascinating. Outside, beyond the mesh screen, the leaves on the trees look so very green.

We sit up and realize it's starting to hit—things are shifting in scale and leaving after-effects, echoes, trails of themselves in my vision. Priya leaves to go to the bathroom, and I look at the wall. There: a pattern in the soft of the white; paisley, maybe. Leaning in for a closer look, it disappears. Then I look at the portraits of Nia, in all of them, her face obscured. In one, she is asleep. Pale blue bed sheets rippled against her milky, soft back. In another, she faces a mirrored medicine cabinet, slightly askew so that the camera does not catch her reflection. Inside, the medicine bottle labels are hard to read. I think one of them says citalopram. All these portraits center around her solar yellow hair.

Priya is suddenly back in the room and closes the door. She keeps repeating how she doesn't like it being open because the draft makes it creak.

We lie down on the bed together again; start talking about shapes on the ceiling; moth-like eyes, Alex Grey structures, "Tool album covers" (Nia's words). Priya says her blood is "like LaCroix" and, like this was the funniest thing I have ever heard, I double over laughing.

Priya says it's comfortable to have contact, so I hold her hand. It feels cold, clammy. Like toad skin. She breathes deep and says, "mmm, yeah." She says, "mmm, yeah" a lot.

I ask her to cuddle me and she does. I'm facing the mirror and tell Priya my reflection has wings: light and mighty; tall, champagne wings. She asks if I can feel them, the breeze against them, but I can't.

She stands and draws the curtains. Likes it better in the dark. This makes things suddenly much worse for me. The pink curtains make the room dark, reddish, womb-like. So, so muggy. I can't breathe very well. I tell Priya this and she says she can get a fan. She disappears to get Nia and I lie down on the bed alone. Every time I open my eyes, Priya and Nia blip around the room like forest sprites.

The mugginess and weird distortions feel suddenly too much. I don't know how much time has elapsed but I don't like it and want to get off. I start to dry-heave. I cover my mouth when I look at them. It must seem like I'm elated by the sight of their love, their tender display of affection, but really, I'm trying to stave off a panic attack. Priya lies back down, Nia loitering by the door, saying she could go but it feels nice to stand around. I begin to panic. When Nia leaves and Priya comes back, she holds me. I complain that I want to get off the ride. That I did too much. I feel, for some reason, trapped in this childhood home, and I don't like experiencing time and space in this weird, dreamlike state. Even lying down, closing my eyes is no reprieve; I can't sleep. It's a constant state of wakefulness that splits me across time, trapped in this room, this moment, and I'm terrified it will last forever.

I ask Priya what time it is. She hesitates, then tells me it's 2:00 p.m.

Which means that it's been an hour. One. Hour. Hysteria blooms out of me like a bloodied cut. How the hell has it only been *one* fucking hour? The news sets me off completely—it feels both like it has been a few hours but also days? Years—? Like I've been in Priya's room since she was a kid. I get up off the bed and things look too big—I'm a kid and everything is so, so big. Priya asks if I want to go outside on the balcony. I trust her. She feels like an older sister. I just want so badly to feel better, so we go outside together. Nia suggests chairs, but I just curl up with my arms around my knees and look through the barriers out at the trees.

For a while, I'm stuck in this infinite backyard, too. Priya comes and goes, bringing me a sweater, a blanket. I lie down in her lap, fetal. Scared. So scared. Priya strokes my hair and says comforting things. When I look at her hands, her skin looks weird—too textured, dark, spotted. Scary. I ask where my mom is, and she says she loves me very much. I repeatedly thank her.

"You're so nice," I whisper through tears. "So sweet. Like a big sister." I feel bad that her trip is being spent so central to keeping me afloat. I feel awful. I want to cry.

We head back inside and I collapse across the kitchen floor. Nia's cat, Kimchi, curls up against me, perching herself overtop of my legs. This entire time I'm in my underwear and a sweater. Here and again, Priya lies beside me. I don't know where she is, but her hair is so soft. She is stroking me and this is comforting.

"I've committed unforgivable shit," I say. The levity of these moral crimes feels all too real to me, but still, Priya says she forgives me. She kisses my tears and her lips are rough as unhewn rock. "I forgive you."

Then: a shift, from this scary time-duality to something else—I'm trying to remember me, and the world, and all the things in it, but I can't. I can only remember blips, and anything that contextualizes it, me, a place, a memory—I cannot fathom. It doesn't come. It just won't. I start talking a lot. I'm chatting so much. I'm reeling in the things I've done, the people I've met.

And Priya and Nia are listening to all of this with such intent. I can't see them, still lying on the ground, staring at their ceiling lamp, shaped like the half-moon of a breast. Nia is cooking. I realize I'm crying. A lot. Tears are just flowing down my face, and I say certain things and my face contorts almost painfully and I start crying so much. I'm so congested, they get me tissues, and I leave them scattered across the floor like paper flowers. I think about how in love they are with each other, how perfect they are for one another, and this, too, makes me cry. I like that they are listening to all this, me chatting nonstop. The tears come, but by then it's more elating. Priya dabs tiger balm on my face, stroking at my arms and my hair. Although her skin is rough and spotted, it feels nice.

We talk like this until I'm starting to feel time a little more linear, gradually, until it's back to normal. It's around 6:30 or 7:00 p.m. After this, we watch some ghost hunting with Nia and order some pizza. We all sit on the couch together. I scroll through Criterion Channel and read synopses. Then we go out for a long walk. Priya and Nia walk together and kiss but it doesn't bother me, when usually, it would. I have a migraine coming on, so when we get back, I take a couple Klonopin and fall asleep in a sea of Priya's stuffed animals with her smiling down on me, benevolent, with the morning sun backlighting the silhouette of her golden hair like a halo.

III

Dreams. Like blood rushing. Raccoon roadkill, pelt all smeared across the street in a shaggy pink-grey pulpy paste of muscle and blood-encrusted fur. In the dream, I take it home. I try to embalm it but when I look down, I'm pumping formaldehyde into my own arteries and I wake. The nightmare bleaches with the morning; fading to absurd gestures and vignettes, though it leaves me thinking of taxidermy, so on Priya's day off we go to the Old Cavern boutique. It's a creepy little shop with a selection of curiosities, specimens and, most importantly, taxidermy. The walls there are painted that shade of New Age purple that looks best in a penumbra. Seeing it in the daytime, like this, they reflect the light making the place look cheap and dirty. Like a sex dungeon or a strip club with the house lights on. It's got that malodorous stench that reeks of bottom-shelf tequila from ethanol-based cleaning supplies. There're just some places that shouldn't be touched by day. At least they keep it clean, I guess.

As we walk through, Priya drags her hand over the surface of things like a sea creature, sensing through touch. She picks things up with mild interest and I record clips of her on my cell phone for my short film while she's not looking. Her long, sharp nails painted a verdant green, grazing over bones and pointing a porcupine quill at me like she's casting a spell. I grab a rodent femur and we play-fence a little. This place closes at six anyhow, so we only get a moment to stroll through the rooms, every flat surface tastefully cluttered with delicate gold-painted framings of cicadas, skulls and stuffed bodies of every animal imaginable, flanked by glass apothecary jars filtering the light through coiled snake corpses. Priya pockets some African porcupine quills in an empty room. I get enticed by a malachite pendant and pay at the front. The woman at the cash desk smiles kindly and tells me, as she's wrapping it in black tissue that reeks of that factory-plastic smell, that malachite has healing properties to balance mood swings.

Priya says it's a toxic stone. Carcinogenic, I think, is the word she uses.

"Gwyneth Paltrow told women it reduced menstrual cramps, or was a coochie-cleanser or some such shit, and this one-percenter subscriber of her bullshit had a polished bathtub carved of it and they fucking died from toxic exposure."

"I was just on my way to lick all the crystals at the crystal store." I pocket my credit card and thank the woman behind the desk.

As we leave, Priya looks at me a little sad. "I read somewhere that more lapidaries and miners die from carcinogenic exposure working with malachite than any other gemstone in the world."

"Okay," I laugh defensively. This doesn't seem like my problem. Overly saccharine displays of sentimentality. What can I, in Montreal, on a Thursday afternoon, do to fight for the cause? I am, just like you, in a constant frenzied state between the doghouse and the lion's den. Maybe I kneel and worship at the church of leisure. So sue me. Fighting for humanity et al. Not my jam. Do I fantasize about not having a phone and being out in some third world country helping people build mud huts? No, I don't. The news moves so fast these days, I can barely keep up with my own city. I say my piece. "You want me to return it?"

"No." I can't read the look she gives me. She shrugs and pulls out her phone. "I'm just saying. We need to stop romanticizing this woo woo shit."

Just then, a Co-Star astrology app badge drops down from the head of her phone screen. Daily affirmations. Today's divine intervention squatting out a fat turd in the shape of a question mark.

Co-Star says: Your Day At A Glance:

You always have a choice

She turns it to face me, giving a stupid grin.

"Oh, what, you're only down for woo-woo shit when it's convenient for you, huh?"

"I didn't say nothin'."

"Fuck off." I shove her shoulder, a little harder than I intend to. Still, she grins. I do a 180 and march my ass back into the crystal shop.

"Did you get my text?" Nia is standing from the couch when we walk in. Her laptop is sitting on the coffee table, for the first time not blaring ghost hunters, but something else. The words *terrible tragedy* and *isolated incident* blare from its speakers. I don't know why, but my first thought is a school shooting.

Priya heel-steps her shoes off. "Is everything okay?"

I'm pulling my sneakers off, looking between the two of them. Priya's face is a taught, pale mask.

Look, Nia saying: *It's so fucked up.*

And it is.

She's got MTL Blog pulled up on her beat-up laptop covered in half-peeled band stickers, a bunny with demonic eyes, and a bumper-sticker style one across the back that reads *Worship the void!* and there are two headlines: one that says something about a guy beating his friend to death, and another about a rare case of cannibalism.

It's not someone we know, but Nia still seems legitimately upset by this.

I go into the other room and pull up Twitter. Explore feeds flooded with local news. I don't know why but this doesn't surprise me as much as it should. Montreal's so fucked up. Between Polytechnique and Luka Magnotta, nothing surprises me about what happens here anymore. I open the article and the headline strobes against my eyes.

Montreal Police Arrest Man Suspected of Killing, Eating 5-Year-Old Son.

Oof.

The headline photo is yellow police tape.

I have to swap to online forums before I can find any photos of the guy. He looks normal enough. Of course, news outlets are always so generous when posting photos of white crime. Fuckers.

I pinch to zoom in on the photo to get a closer look. Come to think of it, he kind of looks familiar. The dad of someone I know? My own dad's coworker? I rack my brain for clues. Scroll scroll scroll. A lil' more.

And then, finally, an article with his name.

Holy shit.

"Priya?" I yell.

"Yeah?"

"Get in here."

I can hear the floorboards creak as she pushes herself off of Nia and strides across the apartment.

I swivel my phone on my desk to face her.

"Tell me this is just some weird coincidence."

Priya's expression twists as she takes in the image with the headline. Her eyes darken.

It's him. Gilbert McNutt. The guy from the trial, in there to put food on the table for his kid. Looks like he found food for the table somehow after all. Sorry, sorry, sick joke.

"I mean, that is really fucking weird, but yeah, it has to be."

I don't know what to say, or if I believe her. It's almost exciting, something this bizarre happening around us. How close could it get?

Priya leans back on her heels, then adjusts her posture. She tugs at the shirt fabric across her abdomen, as though to give her skin more room to breathe and I think I see a shape there, but just liken the motion to a moment of self-consciousness.

"Damn. RIP, Junior McNutt," she says finally.

"What about you?" My stare travels up. I'm looking at her now, hunting the mask of her face for some biological betrayal. Do her pupils shine a disturbing opalescence? "You been feeling okay? Since the trial."

Her gaze jumps up from my phone to my face. Her expression unreadable, a dark cloud shifting over the look in her eyes.

"Yeah," she says. "Just the usual. Upset tummy, insomnia." Then, "Oh," she says.

"Oh?"

"There's also this . . . unbridled rage I . . . can't seem to contain since that day . . . " she changes her voice so it's all distorted and low and demonic. "I think . . . I feel it coming on now . . . oh no—"

"Priya—"

"I'm feeling . . . extra hungry . . . " coming around the back side of my chair, now, and me, going, *no, Priya—NO. Down. Bad Priya.* And her, ignoring this, fingers extending like thin brown fronds. "Hungry for some *brains* . . . ?"

Nia; thin, ominous voice from the next room over: *they're coming to get you, Luca . . .*

And the pillar of Priya's shadow falling over my face; big, stupid grin, hands raining down on me like spiderlings, in my hair and the crook of my neck, squealing like a slaughterhouse pig, not sure just exactly how funny that wording is now, but all the other stuff—the news and the real cannibalism—already gone and forgotten.

IV

Nosebleeds, nightmares, spasms in her sleep. And that's just at night. In the daytime, Priya edits footage of herself from the night before, jerking against the bedsheets, a rank, wet mess. I try to peek over her shoulder at the sped-up recordings from the kitchen where I wash dishes.

Every passing hour, she's looking more and more like a broken doll, slumped against a pile of pillows, her jacket draped across her legs. The first week of the trial where everything was peachy is now like a long-faded dream. I'm still on the placebo and Priya's still taking her horse pills, her weekly injections. Part of me doesn't feel so bad. Misery loves company, and all that. I wonder if underneath, maybe, she's started to atomize and disintegrate. She spends almost all her time either in the bathroom, her bedroom, or out at shows. She's still writing herself notes, like an errand list. I find them around the apartment. Symptoms and snatches of words, fragments. The selection seems arbitrary. As though she's fumbling for purchase onto an already-fading film still; grains of sand sifted between fingers, which vanish on the wind.

We get a survey from the clinic. Their server is down so they've sent a paper one in the mail. One of those *please select all that apply* questionnaires printed on clinic-branded letterhead.

In the last week, I've experienced the following symptoms as a result of B-13-AIL medication (please check all that apply):

Issues with impulse control
Suicidal thoughts

Binge eating
Nosebleeds
Incontinence
Involuntary muscle movement
Acute/unexpected aggression or irritability
Somnambulism (sleepwalking)
Other (describe in detail)
None

I check off the last box, marked *"None"*, fold the piece of paper back up and slip it into the pre-paid return envelope.

When Priya goes to take a leak, I peek at hers. She has a stellium of symptoms. Wow. All the boxes except mine have been checked off. Even the one just above mine—*Other*, followed by a blank line—has been filled.

On it, she's added one last one that's been crossed out and replaced with another: ~~cancerous lesions~~ *deep ulcer/cavity appeared on abdominal wall. hungry.*

V

Next evening, real casual, passing my phone back and forth to Priya—just her and I, Nia out somewhere with her friends. Deciding on pizza toppings and whether or not folding a pizza in half makes it a taco, when I try to offhandedly mention the ulcer.

"So, what'd you put down on the survey . . . for the symptoms?"

And, "god," she rubs her temples. "Like, all of them. And I bet you have none."

"Yeah." Looking around the room, the kind of thing a cat does when it knows you want attention and it's trying to pretend it's considering its options. "I kinda peeked at yours."

"Luca . . . "

"What's up with the hole on your chest? The pocket pussy."

Priya lowers the phone, gives me that deadpan look of hers that screams Roz from *Monsters, Inc.* "It's not a pocket pussy."

"It sure sounds like a pocket pussy."

She looks back down at the phone, scrolling through topping options. "It's like a . . . I don't know, it's just soft. More like a mouth. I was writing the other day on a notepad and fell asleep with it on my chest and when I woke up it was gone."

"What? It just—disappeared into it? Like, 'sorry, teacher, my pocket pussy ate my homework' disappeared?"

"Well, fuck, when you put it that way. Yeah, I guess. I don't know how to explain it." Her hand moves to the hem of her shirt like she's about to lift it, then settles there, playing with the loose stitching. "I thought maybe I'd just misplaced the notebook, but . . . this is going to sound fucked, but I've tried to put things inside."

"Inside . . . the ulcer? What kinds of things?"

"Like, alive things. Like a Venus fly trap eating insects, or whatever. I know that sounds fucking deranged, but remember the ALS trial we did last year when you started to get little bumps in your mouth?"

"Yeah," I say. "I remember." God, that shit hurt so bad. The little ulcers connected into one giant ulcer and I had to check out of the trial early with half-pay because I couldn't handle the side effects. They popped like cysts and out flowed a milky pus that infected all down my throat and stopped me from eating, swallowing, *speaking* without this searing pain. I was swallowing banana-flavoured steroidal liquids for weeks after that.

"It's . . . I don't know. I don't want to freak you out. It kind of freaks me out. Sometimes it looks like it's scabbing over, then other times it looks like it's deepening, like a dark red mouth stretching my navel wide."

It both does and doesn't freak me out. It's oddly elating—this sense that *something* is happening, like a content warning before a graphic video—and I can't seem to shake the danger alarm blaring in my head.

"Can I see? Does it bite?"

Her demeanor changes. I can sense her closing herself off.

"No. What? No."

"Why?"

"'Cause that's like asking to see someone's genitals, you can't just ask someone to see their pocket pussy."

"So, it is a pocket pussy."

"Shut up, Luca."

She passes me the phone after her pizza selection, and I take a moment to make my own. After checkout, I look at her. Really look at her. I'm trying to read something in her eyes, testing how much she'll comfortably share before she closes herself off completely. That's always an inevitability with Priya. You have to take the truthful conversations when they come, milk them for all they're worth, because once she's done talking about a subject, you can bet there would be no cracking that vault until she decides she wants it back open.

"You're cool with staying on it?"

"I need the money."

"I know." I wish I could help. I could. I could offer her my money, or part of it. But then I get this flare up of how that's not fair and the thought slams closed like a steel casket. And then, "We can swap, if you want. You can take the placebo."

"They're gonna know."

The corner of my mouth tightens. "How would they know?"

"Luca . . ."

It's not like we haven't tried this before. The ole switcheroo. They can always tell. Sometimes they don't care. I'm banking that this time they won't care.

"What if they don't care?"

"I can't risk it this time. I'm paying down student debt and finishing this will just put me over the edge for my flight to Helix in San Francisco. Just a couple more weeks left. I'll be fine."

Right. Helix. Priya's golden ticket to a world of networking, filmmaking, and stardom. Goodbye, pizza nights. Goodbye, clinical trials. Goodbye, Luca.

I try to correct my thoughts; they feel overly dramatic, but this one thing implants itself in me like a weed in a garden. Taking root, threatening to overtake the flowers Priya and I have together tended there. I'm worried someday it'll fruit; multiply, send off little carrier seeds like dandelion fluff across the landscape of my mind, and my jealousy will flood me like a plague and eat away at our friendship until there's nothing left. We'll be just acquaintances, someone I'll say I once knew, a long time ago, back before she was someone who was anyone.

VI

Hello self-loathing, my old nemesis. I'm on Twitter in the middle of the night. Diazepam and zolpidem cocktail's not really working. I can feel that I'm fucked up from the meds, but it's not enough to put me to sleep, and the trial meds—being placebo and all—have no effect on my sleep cycle. Instead, I'm just floating around in this jet-lagged state of *bleh*. Kinda writing notes down from the trial on the notes app, kinda half-masturbating. I don't have anything solid to go off of, so it's pretty touch and go. For the writing, I mean. It'd be different if it weren't placebo. Right now, I'm just hunting through Erowid Vault for drug symptoms. I could always ask Priya. God knows I've been filming her enough to make up a short film.

A flare of jealousy detonates in my chest. I try not to let it cloud my thoughts.

I put my phone away under my pillow. Close my eyes and try to sleep.

Cars drift by outside, the city's ocean waves waxing gently in and out, tethered to their own secret lunar cycles. The bathroom pipes behind the wall to the right of me hum out a little hymn.

Fifteen minutes pass like this and then my eyes snap open. I stare at a bunch of shapes in the hall: the sofa, a garbage bag leaning up against a side table.

Feels like there's an electric current running through me. Well, I think, if I can't sleep, I might as well doom-scroll.

I reach impulsively for my phone again, pull it out and prop myself up on my pillow.

When I look up and out from my room into the hall, there's a silhouette that wasn't there before. Statuesque, unmoving. I squint my eyes, trying to decipher what it is. Drop my phone into my lap and when I blink to rub my eyes, and the shape looks bigger, or closer—I'm not sure which. A vague shadow playing a game of Red Light, Green Light by itself in the dark. It looks like a chewed-up bubblegum amoeba. The shape shivers, inky black against the backdrop of the equally murky hallway and I think I see the shape of a hand, an arm.

"Priya?"

It shifts. The profile silhouette jerks towards me—towards my sound—in savage animal movement.

I sit frozen. I'm actually frightened, a little bit. It is Priya, but something about her is wrong. Her body made unfamiliar.

She moves in slow, languid steps towards the kitchen and her form disappears from within the door frame.

I grab my phone and tap the screen. Its light crashes against my eyes, illuminating the room a sickly white. It is 3:05 a.m.

I slip out of bed, cautious as to not make a sound. Impulsively grab my digicam—almost out of juice but on, thank fuck—and creep down the hall to our kitchen overlooking the living room, a sparse couch. I don't see anyone, but the apartment door is open and Priya has slipped out like a nocturnal animal.

I slide on my sneakers and follow her out.

Maybe it's a trick of the light but her torso looks misshapen, elongated; stretched by some unseen sculptor's hand. I hadn't realized—or maybe she'd been better at hiding it than I thought, not quite letting on the severity of what's been happening to her body—but, for the first time, the trial drugs feel not just strange but dangerous.

Her body moves in somniferous, danceresque motions. As she swings her arms to walk in slow, exaggerated motions, there is a gentle rosined sound: the skin-on-fabric of her pyjamas. Her hair falls flat upon her shoulders and dances across her back. I lift the camera and start recording from the back. In the dark, the ISO grain is high, shapes barely visible against the background. I want to flick on my phone flashlight to compensate, but then think better of it; I don't want to wake her. I surge past her down the hall to come around the front of her, where I start to take backwards steps, filming her face, her features dark, sweat-glazed wounds.

I am no longer myself, her expression seems to say.

But what is she, then?

I lead her out of the basement apartment onto the street towards the highway. I can see the inclined top of the Olympic Stadium jutting out into the skyline like a pointed tooth angled up at the moon. I fall behind filming the stadium and have to take a couple quick steps to get ahead of her again, then spin around and start walking backwards so I can get a good look.

Her eyes are glassy and shallow. Huge pupils, big as coins. Sleepwalking.

It's not just her eyes, I realize. There are strange things about her body. The veins across her neck and face are bulging, and—I don't know how to explain it—it's almost like I can see the outline of her spine from the front of her. She's wearing a cropped shirt with a cherub riding a horse on it, stopping just above her abdomen. There're the vertical beads of her spinal column, I count four of them, *one, two, three, four*, and when I'm staring at her neck for a closer look to see if it continues its bloom against her ribcage, I hear a crushing sound, but wet.

We both stand still.

I look around with the camera and then down. Priya has leaned back onto her left foot, raising the other from a brown, murky stain on the road.

Underfoot, I glimpse a terrifying image: under Priya's bare foot is a small, brown animal, half-crushed from being hit by a car. I think of the roadkill nightmare from the day we went to the clinic. It looks something like that, but smaller. A rat or a marmot. It's mostly face up, wretched little arms curled inward like it's tiptoeing along the two-dimensional viewer field of the pavement. Its insides have been mashed outward, a pulpy ooze of brain matter and viscera unspooling from out its mouth and ass. When I take a closer look, it's taking sickly little wheezes, still alive but just barely.

Oh, fuck. My stomach clenches. Acid crawls up the back of my throat.

Priya's foot presses down, closes over it. Not altogether soft, I can hear a *crunch* as it folds under her weight. It screeches, its tiny high-pitched body letting out its last breath. The air starts to taste of iron, of blood. Her flesh suctions around its body. Makes a tight seal, absorbing it, her calve disappearing into red-violet bubbles. I close my eyes and look away, but I can still hear it—am filming it, too—that wet squelch and the thing screaming, muffled and distorted, and then it stops.

Piss runs down her leg and onto her bare foot, against the mush of fur.

And then, like nothing's just happened, she begins walking again, drunkenly off-kilter and down the road, her bare foot leaving dark stains against the pavement.

There's almost nothing left behind of the little creature. The shaggy outer layer of skin, pulp-mulch, and a femur or a tail, but the bulk of it is gone. Absorbed into Priya's foot. I can hardly believe what it is I've just seen. This has gotta be some Ambien-fueled nightmare. I look up to see where Priya's gone and—

there the sudden glare of headlights whose fluorescence seems scaldingly bright. I jerk forward and snatch the neck of Priya's shirt and tear her back just as a truck rips by.

We tumble back over each other and down into a gravel ditch which scrapes my palms and knees. My camera drops off somewhere in the grass. It's too dark to see where. Priya blinks. Her eyes look newly born.

"Luca?" she says.

My hands are trembling, trying to string together the oiled bits of memory. I don't understand what's just happened.

We feel each other breathe and see by touch in the dark. After some time, I reach for Priya's hand and pull her to stand. She towers over me.

"What just happened?"

I tell her she was sleepwalking. "You almost walked into oncoming traffic."

She asks why I didn't wake her up before then.

"I wanted to see where you were going."

Innocent enough, and true. My neck is starting to ache from looking up, so I turn and start to head back home. I leave the camera in the grass. I'll get it tomorrow. I can't bring myself to tell her about the rest quite yet.

VII

By Tuesday, there's a guy on the news who's slit his own throat. When we recognize him as another clinical trial patient, I dial up the clinic.

It rings and goes to voicemail. I call the emergency line, and then the adjoining university line, who patches me to one of the doctors. No one is answering their calls.

Priya stops taking the medication and she gets all jaundiced and vomits nothing but gastric juices, so she goes back to her prescribed dose the day after.

Three days later, a secretary calls me back. She tells me all the doctors turned off their phones after they went on vacation, but that they should be back in a week. The lead, Dr. Layton, will be in Australia for another two weeks. It's best to avoid going to the ER because they don't know what we've been taking, so they're unequipped to help. Cool. No one cares. Good to know. Clinic report card rating? F, for "Fucked."

I'm increasingly on-edge around Priya. She's doing shit that pisses me off and I don't want to bring any of it up because it feels petty, even though it festers in me like a cancer. It erodes at my mood. I feel like she's replacing me with her new friend Robin, who has seemingly burst onto the stage of our lives out of nowhere. They met online on some indie movie forum, then in person, and since then have been inseparable. I wonder how much Priya's told her about the trial, our involvement, and her films. I wonder if she's shown Robin clips I haven't seen. I wonder if they'll collaborate. I need that thought like a hole in the head. Once it's there it sets me off, and I end up so irrationally wound-up by it that I wake up with a migraine the next day from being so tense all night.

At the end of the week, I go back and scavenge the side of the road, kicking through tall sun-bleached grass 'til I find my digicam. It's dead, but in otherwise fine condition. When I get home, I charge it and boot up my computer. I take notes and replay the footage. I still cannot fathom what it is I've seen. There, clear as day, is the footage from the other night. Priya sleepwalking. Priya stepping on some kind of rodent that scuttled across the road and paralyzed itself with proximate fear. Priya's foot closing over its little body. Priya's foot absorbing the animal like a carrion vulture. She's in the next room, and the thought lights in my mind, flint-quick, that I should tell her. Maybe. Maybe. Don't be so wishy-washy. I can show her after. After what? After I cut it into something, of course.

I import the clips into a video editor, close my bedroom door, and get to work.

VIII

Two days later, *duh duh duh*, nothing's going on.

All the food around us is spoilt, but I'm not sober long enough to make proper mental note of why. Plants, too. I also can't figure out where Nia's cat, Kimchi, has disappeared off to. Priya told me it's not even hers, it's just some neighbour's cat who comes rolling round from time to time.

The day I've planned to talk to Priya about her sleepwalking incident, show her the footage I've compiled into something vaguely artistic, she tells me she's planned for us to go to a rave, and I put it off. Don't want to kill the buzz.

That night the moon is a pale glass marble, high in the sky.

Robin shows up with a taxidermy mouse for Priya. It's wearing a little cowboy hat and chaps. Holding a little pistol all right with both its tiny little hands extended.

"I found it dumpster diving," she says. "I'm a fucking klepto."

Priya seems enamoured, though her face is sallow. The yeehaw mouse goes on the living room bookshelf, front and center. I don't think I've ever made Priya anything that's gone on her shelf front and center. The image of the crushed rat soaking up into Priya's foot strobes against my eyelids. I cringe and look askant.

Robin has a whole aesthetic. 2000s raver girl, flare pants, whale tail. All they talk about is her boyfriend. I try to distract myself, popping fruit strips into my mouth. There's sixteen in a pack. I think I can fit maybe ten in my mouth at a time before I stop chewing. When the taste disappears, I toss the Pepto-pink lump in the trash and unwrap another.

There's a knock at the door and Robin's skinny boyfriend, Rhys, explodes into the room.

"Who wants to get fucking pie-faced?"

He does a little tap-dance and ends with a flourish; jazz hands. He already looks sloshed.

I say hi, but I don't think he hears. He says he's gonna do ketamine with Nia and Robin. Priya declines. Rhys looks at me like I'm some dumb piece of shit Kimchi dragged in, dropped off, and then offers some to me, like he has to.

I shake my head no, and then I regret it.

"I'll just take shrooms," I say. Enough to give me a pleasant high; champagne bubbles in my blood.

"Okay," he says. His posture slackens and his face floods with relief.

Robin racks the stuff into three lines and snorts it, and I don't think she looks at me for the rest of the night.

Rhys weaves a cigarette between his fingers like a stimming

teen twirling a pen during a math exam while we wait for the time to leave. I scroll through Twitter while they all sit and chat.

"Hey," I say. "Listen, listen. It's about that cannibal last week."

They all go quiet. I don't look at them 'cause I don't want to see the stupid, irritable face Robin and co. are making from my interruption. It's seared into my head without me needing to look.

"Investigators determine that cannibal attacker Gilbert McNutt was under the influence of an antipsychotic clinical trial drug when he killed himself, his wife, and their five-year-old son in the municipality of LaSalle. Bottles of the experimental medication were discovered in his home, and a 150mL vial was found in his pocket, according to the coroner." I look up from my phone.

Rhys makes a twisted face. "Don't tell me that, man. I don't need a fucking downer to freak me out right before I'm about to trip."

They go back to talking about an ambient album Rhys is working on. Robin's going to make the cover art. When I ask how long they plan to be at the rave, it's like no one hears me. They don't say a thing.

Peachy. Feels like a precursor to the rest of the night.

We pass by a house on the way to the metro. Yellow police tape boxes off the exterior. There's a small crowd. A woman in cuffs. A sliver of face peeks out between the curtain of her scraggly hair. Her body is a disjointed wire frame, and the bulk of her abdomen looks . . . *wrong*, somehow. Like it's deflated. I strain my eyes a bit. Maybe a trick of the light, but it's not just deflated, but completely hollow, the edges of her tattered garment an event horizon around a deposit of night. Like, if I step a little to the right to align myself, I'm almost sure I'll look completely through her. Into what? I'm not entirely sure. An EMT sits on the lip of the curb, his head in his hands. Laughing or sobbing, I can't tell which. Another EMS crumbles halfway down the stairs outside the house.

"Oh, fuck—" Nia whispers and I think about what kind of fucked up thing it takes to make an EMT cry.

Rhys must be thinking the same thing 'cause he swivels around on his heels and books it in the other direction.

"Nah, fuck that." He spits, a dark bubbling stain against the concrete. "I'm outta here. This is gonna kill my trip."

He trots off and down the subway station steps, and the rest of us follow. Can't tell if it's the crime scene or the change in environment that makes me feel bad. We file onto the subway, mostly vacant this late at night and far out east, and find some seats.

Short bursts of light blaze across my eyes as we leave the station. The hum-buzz of the subway thrums against my eardrum like the secret hymn of a seashell. A roaring hosanna of white noise.

I look at the others as they sit and talk. Priya and Nia together, and Rhys and Robin. Gotta love being the fifth wheel. I rap my head against the glass window as the stations pass. A corridor of lights wink past me like embroidered lines connecting constellations. My reflection swims in the dark beyond the window. In it, all I see is my ugly. The girl I desperately try to smother, the one who comes clawing back out of the well-deep stratum of self-loathing, caked on thick as treacle every time shame rears its wretched head.

Out somewhere in Montreal East, we are walking for what feels like forever. I am in an inexplicably shitty mood. We trek on a highway and so not to trail behind the others, I try to spark up a conversation with Robin. I ask about how she and Rhys met, and they exchange a knowing look and laugh. She says they met at Club Stereo and leaves it at that.

We get to a massive parking lot, void of cars, and then hop a chain barrier into some woods. There's a couple of teen boys here, too. One of them's putting on a stoner voice, going *"broooo, you gotta try this oxygen shit. Shit is sick, bro. The illest—"* pretending to vape at the air. Robin turns to us, taking a few backwards steps and makes a face and says *"yikes"* and it shuts the teens up and sets us off rolling in laughter.

Rhys has to pull out his cell phone for us to see where we're going in the forest and after what feels like nearly an hour, we come to a drop off into a clearing. There's a little stereo setup and some small LED lights strobing. Barely a crowd. What I could safely say is the first—and lamest—outdoor rave I've ever been to.

Priya feels bad. She tells me repeatedly this isn't what they meant when they said they'd take me to a rave, that they'll make it up to me later when they can find a better one. I ask Rhys about videos of a rave in a sewer I'd seen floating around the web, and he says, "Oh sure. We gatekeep that one from losers, but I can show you."

I try to smile, but it pains me the way he's framed his words.

Couple beers and bright coloured pills get passed around and then everyone starts dancing. The whole time I'm bad tripping. Not sure what's happening to me, I can't see my hands straight. I want to leave, but I don't know how to find my way out of the forest and it's still early. So, I tell myself, take it easy. Chill the fuck out. I brace myself against a tree behind the crowd so as not to get overwhelmed. Last thing I need out here is to have a panic attack. A couple hours watching bodies move and then I can go home.

I close my eyes and wait it out. Ten minutes, twenty. Maybe longer.

Open them back up, and the visual of the crowd still drags me in like a riptide. In the shadows, I can see Priya dancing against Nia. It's more crowded now, and darker, LEDs strobing like a searchlight against a swarm of shadows packed in hot and close. I swim in the edacious beat of the crowd towards them. The dark disfigures them, looking like one body. Priya presses her ass against Nia's pelvis, and they grind together.

The next song fades in, a moody melody underpinned by a nimble baseline. While I watch them dance, I listen a little more closely. The singer is seductively crooning, and the baseline grows, expansive, adds syncopated, heavy drumbeats that make the whole thing roll smooth as an 18-wheeler.

When she sees me, Priya breaks free and reaches for my wrist. She smiles and ushers me in, tries to get me to dance with them. Presses my body between them, pinning me to Nia. I pull away. Wet blanket on a down, and Priya makes a weird face, what I interpret to be a half-annoyed, half-disappointed look, and melts back into the shadowy sky of bodies to dance with Nia. I withdraw, a drifting satellite. Someone shoulder checks me to get closer to the DJ and I stumble back on some uneven terrain. Lower on a hill, where all I can see are the black silhouettes of bodies dancing. A new song begins, something low and warped and heady and I'm feeling the shrooms, now, really feeling them, and the nausea hits me like a thunderclap. I try to push through the bodies, to move myself towards the clearing, but there's too many people. My hands slip against sweaty skin, and I dry heave. I collapse onto my knees and try to focus on something grounding. God—anything. My hands look all fucked up, so I can't look at those. Up, instead, and there's a woman standing by a tree with her panties pulled aside, urinating on a guy's face. The loose shape of another woman walks up to her and starts laughing hysterically. Back and away, up at Priya and Nia and I see the glimpse of something wet against her abdomen, dark and glistening. She's pushing Nia's hands into it, like a dark, open womb. The cloying reek of dying white flowers assaults my senses.

The sight knocks me back, winded, and suddenly my trip takes a turn for the worst.

All the black silhouettes of bodies dancing and writhing against me, thick and heavy with sweat, whirring lights past me like a dive through Kubrick's Stargate, yellow streamers with blooms of white against a dense, black canvas. I gotta get out of here, somewhere less temporal. I grab my phone and—I know it's a bad idea. I know I shouldn't be looking at my phone high on shrooms and hopped up on god knows what else, but I do, I do—I pull up Twitter and a tweet beams into my eyes in crystal clear vision, no dark mode needed, phone hot against my hand like an electric spark and I've read it before I can even really register what it is that I'm looking at.

@PriyaBathory: Wrapping up my next short film. It's about a clinical trial of DMT gone wrong. All vibes, no plot. A lil' excerpt clip below, as a treat.

And below, a video. A plunge into grainy darkness, crackling white noise. I can't help but watch, just a little excerpt; Priya's signature cinematography and subtitled poetic prose, this lyricism that cannot be contained or duplicated, that feels somehow like every word rings true; like none of them could be replaced, because the music of it is a garden she's been tending to her whole life. On an island. In the stars. On another planet. I don't know. All I know is, Priya's been writing LiveJournal diary entries, zines, and ethereal lyrics since she was a kid, and it shows. When you hone a craft for so many years, it *shows*, and there's this yearning in me, I wish I could have it. I want to bottle it like a firefly, eat it raw and puke it back up with my name on it, all of this against uniquely minimalist landscapes of otherworldly textures of indigo; an upside-down shot, the backlit silhouette of her in our bathroom injecting the meat of her thigh with the medication.

And the worst part of it is, it's gone pretty viral. Viral-ish, viral *enough* so that people see it and associate it with her, and I feel like my whole fucking world is collapsing in on me. Like I'm thinking about my clinical trial hanahaki thing and how it's kind of smooth-brained, no plot, worse: no vibes, and how there can't be two shorts so similar out there—not from two people so close, not from us, and a rage builds in me, in need of direction.

I can feel it bubbling up out of me.

Oh, god.

Something in me unhinges.

I stand up shakily and seek Priya out of the crowd like a heat missile, then make my way towards her.

Nia's fucked off somewhere, so I don't have to worry about censoring myself. I fling the phone around with the Twitter clip like it's hotel receipts from my spouse's affair. I stomp up to Priya and shove it in her face. The phone light blares against her eyes, and she winces.

"Are you fucking kidding me? You're making a short about the clinical trial? *Why?* When were you going to tell me?"

No one's looking 'cause the music is so loud, and I'm thinking *good* because I need that kind of anonymity right now. The rage in me feels vacuous.

"What?" she says. *What? What?* Her voice echoes in my mind in mocking imitation, inane echolalia. Can't tell if she really doesn't know or didn't hear, either way, forcing me to repeat myself makes me turn a spotlight onto how inane it all sounds, but I can't stop. It's like the feeling has tumbled up my throat and has nowhere to go but out my dumb-ass mouth.

"Why not?" she says finally, looking down at my phone. The fact that she's still dancing, rotating her shoulder-blades into the skin of strangers, heightens my irritation.

"Because *I'm* making a film about it. You *knew* that I was making a short about it."

"You said you were doing, like, a hanahaki story," she blurts.

"Yeah, based *on the trial experience*. It was like—the whole *impetus* of even doing the fucking trial." I'm fuming. My hands are balled into fists and my jaw is set. I want to bash her fucking face in. I feel like I'm barely keeping my rage contained. "When did you decide you were going to film something?"

"What do you mean? I've been jotting notes since day one."

"What do you mean?" I parrot her voice back at her. Jotting notes. Like it's a side project. A mom's hobby Etsy shop. I spit the words. "In-fucking-credible."

Priya stares at me with dead eyes. Her voice is barely audible above the music, but I can sense the defensive cut in her words.

"It's nothing like yours. It's about genetic memories. Yours is about fungus. Don't even worry about it."

"I'm very fucking worried. You're like ninety percent done and when I finish mine and come out with it, people are going to think I'm imitating you."

"Are you?"

"No?"

"So? There you go. You're way too concerned with what other people think. Just finish what you're writing, it'll be fine."

"It's not like it's a haunted house story, it's about a clinical trial. Which no one does. Except I was *going to*. Because I'm *in* a clinical trial."

"Holy sheep shit, everyone! Luca, who's in a clinical trial experiment—*as a placebo*—thinks he has free fucking reign over the entire body horror sub-genre!" Her eyes are wild—big black saucers which almost obliterate the sclera. "What's this really about? Why are you having such a meltdown?"

"A *meltdown*? You're going to make me look like a fucking moron in front of everybody and you're calling this a meltdown?"

"What do you want me to do? Take it down?"

Yes, I think wildly. *Un-fucking send it*. But also, no. No, I just want it to disappear. I want it to never have happened. I want the file to corrupt and no longer exist. I don't want to be responsible for it.

"No. I don't know."

"Is this about the Helix workshop?"

"What the fuck? No. I don't even care about that." My voice flares defensive.

"You didn't even apply."

Her words stab like an icy dagger into my sternum. In and out. Sharp and fast.

"No. It's not about that. I wouldn't even get in, that's why I didn't apply. I know the quality of my work. But you get all these diversity grants and opportunities, and people love you off the bat—"

"That's why you think I got in? Diversity?"

The shape of Nia weaves through the crowd and materializes next to Priya. Her expression, at first light and blithe, turns to concern. My cheeks flares red.

Priya's mouth twists, sour. "When are you going to pull your head out your own ass for long enough to see there's more going on in life than just what happens to you?"

I'm nodding, but not agreeing with her. Nodding like, *oh, you're so fucking right. You're the queen of right, just wafting along above us all on your righteous, golden throne of rightness bestowing the correctness of the world upon the rest of us.* And she can read it in my expression, because she says, "Oh, right. The only big injustice in life happens when bad things are happening to *you*, right? When things don't go right for little miss rich girl over here."

"Blow me," I say.

"On what?" The words out before she can think to call them back. Eyes growing large like scavenged glass. I look at her with all the hurt in the world.

"I'm sorry," she blurts.

I'm already turning, her hand on my shoulder and me jerking away, stiffening like cured resin. I don't want her to be sorry. I want to take this fight to its natural conclusion. I want her to spit venom. I'm tired of her soft attitude. I want her to be just as pissed at me. I want to hear all the bad things I know she thinks about me so I can confirm what it is I think about myself. Poor, poor Luca. The world knows you're a fraud. And we hate you—barely tolerate you—we all can't wait for you to up and disappear so we can lessen our load.

She says none of this, thinks it, maybe; or I do, at least—about myself, I mean. The shroom trip ending in a sobering walk through the forest, phone as a torchlight, all on my own for what feels like forever until I hit the clearing of the parking lot. No Ubers at this time. I check, again and again. Then, when I'm shivering enough to resolve myself to call a cab, I pull up the Toronto After Dark submissions page and type out my name and contact information. Fuck it. Shit or get off the pot, yeah? I upload the clip I'd filmed of Priya sleepwalking, looking fragile, looking holy, until her foot swells into frame over the small brown animal, and a paste of pink-red viscera oozes out like toothpaste. When I get home, an exhaustion hits me like a wave, and I collapse onto my bed where the world clicks off into sleep.

IX

After this, the film won't take form. My inspiration piddles down to a pathetic dribble. Meanwhile, Priya seems to be living her best life. Every day, I see her tweets; her close friend's list photos of her and Nia out on dates. The public-facing casual pics of her at concerts and modelling or photographing her other friends. Robin. Bibi. Everyone but me. Robin takes over my place in the relationship like a friendly new kitten pushing out a senior cat—viperous and unpredictable, outdistanced by sweet and fun. Fuck Robin. She looks at me like I'm sickening, and I can only imagine the conversations she, Nia, and Priya are having behind my back.

One day while they're gone to a concert, I go on an Ambien and cutting binge at one or two a.m., when sleep doesn't come. My arm is covered in shallow ribs of red that I loosely bandage. My bedroom comes in and out of view in choppy, broken fragments, like radio telegraph messages. Spunk-crusted bedsheets. Half-eaten snacks strewn across the dresser into the forgotten crevice between my bed and the wall, dirty clothes tossed in various piles across the floor; the carpet greyed with cat hair, and of course, the plastic container of placebo trial meds I stopped taking two weeks ago. I peer into the old digicam recorder and take a pass around the room.

I look in the mirror, zooming in on my face, my body in pieces. Ambien-scrying. From beneath the shadows of greasy hair appears the chalky half-moon of my face. I see a wooden girl-shape, a plain and dull nepotist, stupid and rich and white, living and dying in this nowhere city, a shrivelled up nobody. A duplicitous parasite. Small. My face pinches into a hard mask. Suddenly, I become livid. I can't stand this awful divination I've bestowed upon myself, and so I throw a blanket over the mirror. It slips off the frame and when I see myself again—my horrid, distorted face staring back at me, boring a hole through my soul with my own cloudy granite-blue eyes, searching—and I cannot take it. With my free hand, I wrap my fist around a brass candle holder and hurl it across the room at the mirror. The metal forces through and it all shatters like glass hit with a sonic boom, cutting my reflection into a thousand tiny pieces, hairline fractures cutting across my face and neck.

You fucking *bitch*, I hiss; my voice thick and revolted. I can't tell if I'm talking about me or if I'm talking about Priya. Everything felt fine until this.

I turn and stalk away. I'm too outraged to notice where I'm headed until it's too late; I've billowed into Priya's room like a curse and I am standing at her small, pretty dresser covered in small, pretty stickers, topped with small, pretty photos of her small, pretty friends. The digicam hangs from a strap loosely wrapped around my palm. I want to crack the photos into splinters. This whole thing has me spiralling the drain. I can feel it. What is Priya doing right now? Documenting? Hanging? Taking notes, finding words for her narrative paragon? The whole thing makes me vicious with rivalry.

I wield one of the photos in my fist and when I turn to throw it, I spot them. The little vial and plastic bottle of pills, sitting at the corner of her desk. Knocked over. Unimportant. A couple are already empty.

I drop the frame and I go back into my room to retrieve the pill bottle, then walk myself back to Priya's. I'm hardly filming any of this. Shots of stained carpet, gaudy found footage punctured by grunts and the dragging of feet. I swap the contents and the vials of hers for mine.

I pick up the bottle and flood a waterfall of pills off into my palm. I hold them as if a Eucharist, my thumbs passing over their smooth, clear casing. Bring a handful to my mouth in some vile, baseless communion. Then another, and another. And then, when it's mollified me enough to put me to sleep, I sit the camera on my dresser pointed at me, and then I go lie down on the couch and the light of the world switches off into inky black.

Priya and Nia and Robin bring home a slew of people. When I wake, more and more of them are pouring into the apartment, the walls breathing, the rooms hot and muggy with exhalation. I stand up from the couch and the air seems to vibrate with energy. It feels like there's an electric current running through my veins, and I'm famished. I go to get a bite and there's some guy eating by the fridge.

"Sup?" he says.

"What's good?" I open the fridge. It's nearly empty. Nothing but condiments and crisp greens. This is what living with a vegan is like. Fuck. I grab some gluten-free bread. It's got chia and probiotics in it or something. I'm snatching slice after slice and shovelling them into my mouth. Then I pilfer a can of beer and drink like it's a battlefield. I'm trying to do some real damage. Give myself something real to write about. Maybe give Priya something to cry about. One could trade goods for another. Conservation of energy; never lost, only transferred, but it has a price. Everything always has a price.

When I go back into my bedroom, there's a couple kissing on my bed.

"Yo," no patience. "Outta my bed."

Their bodies tumble off of each other and out the door. I crawl into bed, feeling fevered. Beneath the sheets are the pill bottles. I almost forgot I took them. I wonder what it could do to a person, taking that many. A descent into madness? That would be fun. I wonder if it's infectious. How long has the stuff been cookin' in Priya's body? A week—a month? Too late for me now. I've gone and dumped a whole bottle into my system. Time to take this thing to its inevitable conclusion, I think, and seize my hand around the empty bottle, clenching like a broken heart.

Priya says she'll take the excerpt tweet down.

My gaze skitters up and along the concrete wall, mesmerized, where the crude etchings of words, symbols, memories in the language of gesture have manifested from my hand overnight, creeping along the landscape in ink black sharpie. I don't remember writing any of this. I can't tell if Priya sees them, or if she even cares. I've been in bed all day. The camera's been rolling footage of me sleeping until the battery runs dead. Is it the Ambien or the drinking or the trial drug or all of it mashed up together that's getting me so fucked up? I guess this is the madness which awaits me if I don't find a way out. Peachy.

I'm nodding like, yeah, yeah, my head bobbing like a sewing needle. Then my eyes land on her. Priya looks tired and thin. She pulls at her eyelashes compulsively, staring at the shattered mirror. She's wearing an oversized Evangelion tee and shorts that make her long, brown legs look canted and deer-like. Her eyes are almost milky cataract-white, but in her face, there is a searching, as though for a memory.

"No, don't," I say. But I don't apologize.

"It's okay," she says. "I can film something else." I look at her. Standing at the edge of the room's threshold. She coughs into a tissue. It's dark and phlegmy, pitted with amber specks. I'm waiting for something . . . I don't know what. An apology or "I miss you" so that I can reciprocate, but I won't be the one to start that chain reaction.

"I'm sorry," she finally says. Her voice is broken, but voiced nonetheless, that interrupts my thoughts, vacuums them free of discretion and fuck, *fuck*, all I can think of is that I've already gone and done the unthinkable, I've taken her pills—all of 'em, every single one. And worse, I've submitted that film.

"Me too," I say. My eyes glint darkly, and I flash her a Sunday-School smile. I'm trying to be optimistic.

She saunters into my room and sits on the edge of my bed. Stalls for an awkward moment and then reaches over and hugs me. Her touch is sun-warm, silver-hued, engrossing over me like a lighthouse. When I rub her back, I can feel something flowering up her spine. A serpentine shift beneath my fingertips, and for a moment I feel repulsion, but sit, my knees astride her back. She sags against my chest. An explosion of guilt detonates inside me.

"I don't want this. The piss-poor pay and debt."

"I know."

Do you? Do you know?

I draw my finger across her back, map the shape of a face and think back to girlhood; draw-on-my-back sleepover games, *criss-cross applesauce, spiders crawling up your back* . . . and the tracing game—the one where you'd chart words across the canvas of each others' skin. And always, "Can you draw it again?" Because it would mean a free massage. And it was always stupid words for friends: penis, poop; always trying to trace the shapes as clearly as possible to intentionally lose and have it be your turn again, but I would revel in the intimacy of donor or recipient with crushes, tonguing my fingertips across their backs like oil paint, lovingly, hiding spells between letters, the cursive loop of an L for *Luck* into *Love*, like a rotational ambigram.

What is it I am drawing now?

"An angel?" Priya asks. She says it's because she can feel the spread of its wings. For this, tears sting at my eyes. She lies in my lap. She clutches at a glass evil eye pendant around my neck, rolls it across its chain. It rumbles pleasant reverberations through my neck. She looks so fragile here, like that. I feel a swell of affection, like I want to use everything I can to take care of her, a sensation that obliterates my factory setting of militant narcissism. When did it stop being like this? When did everything else become all that much more important than it?

"I'm scared of all this."

"The trial?" She doesn't say anything, so I prod. "You want to drop out?"

To this she doesn't answer. She only says, "Don't leave me alone." And my voice hitches with good humour when I hear this.

"I'm not going anywhere." I lean down and plant a kiss on Priya's temple.

She tilts her head back on my lap and looks up. She smiles. That perfect Botticelli smile.

I don't have the strength to tell her what it is that I've done.

I try to load the Twitter page, but it's gone.

Hmm . . . this page doesn't exist. Try searching for something else.
Refresh.
Sorry, that tweet has been deleted.
Refresh.
Sorry, that tweet has been deleted.

My heart feels like it's dangling from a piano string. I feel so bad. No more drawing angel wings. No more of that shroom trip. It's like I've forgotten about it, about all the good moments we've had together. That time our friend Val photographed us for an editorial on friendship, our hair intertwined into a single braid. I've already taken her meds. All of them. I've already taken all of her fucking meds, and replaced them with mine, and I filmed her, and I submitted it for public scrutiny. Sooner or later, she's going to find out.

A little more than two or three days after and a wound, like a mouth, like the one Priya has, appears on my stomach. A seam in me, where something spills through. It ekes its lips out from my navel, a twisted little Möbius strip of flesh growing deep, cavernous; dark and wet.

On the outside, it doesn't have a smell. It doesn't make a sound.

I worship it like a shrine. I shoot Polaroids and videos, feeding food, drugs and small objects—plastic bottle caps and safety pins—into its small purple mouth. I call it Little Luca.

Plunging my fingers down its pale throat. A shiver of fullness, of immense pleasure. Inside, it carries the reek of blood that, over time, grows worse. Rotten. Foul.

I can hear it gurgling, gluttonous.

I hop into the shower and pull off my clothes. Look down and stretch it open like I'm donning a pair of tights.

Within it is an arcing black and crimson vortex with a cut-out center that I can't reach like a side-show game, one you presumably stick your hand into, like an oversized nylon mesh finger-trap, reaching just enough into my belly that one would be sure to trap their arm. And, well, I can only be that belligerent dickhead who sticks something inside, just far enough to skirt the edge of that deeper chasm. Eventually I slide a silicone toy in, and when I do, I shake my head. I can't stop laughing.

Why is everyone's first thought when they find a hole, "Can I fuck it?"

"Who's up for a tarot reading?"

Priya's face is half-bemused as Nia dumps her backpack's contents: an unwinding thread of books and half-eaten snacks and the thick *thump* of a brick-shape against her lap. It is covered with a finely embroidered piña cloth. Always pink. Everything pink. A blushing cherub of youth, flush and ripe against the grey of this apartment.

She positions an old Garfield plushy with worn-away eyes, the shimmering magician's assistant, by her side, and unfolds the cloth carrying the deck. The cards bloom against the pale of her hands, long nails tickling across their gilded edges. I've set up the camera not far off so that it's pointed at us. Our backdrop is a painting of Robin's. I don't like her much, but her work itself is a masterpiece. It looks almost ritualist in its overarching designs. The empirical diagram of some ancient alien temple.

"Luca?"

"How about you do one for all of us?" I say.

Nia nods as she shuffles.

"What's a Christian have to say about divination, Luca?" Priya says.

"The Christian says the world is noisy and we are deaf to most of it. The Christian says faith is a gift from god."

"Of course," Priya says. Her tone is blithe. She's been sick these last few days, presumably from me swapping her medication for my placebo, but I haven't had the heart to say anything. I keep accumulating lies by omission like a magpie stocking treasure, like I might build a nest or a castle out of them all, and wall myself off from the truth of the world.

What this tarot reading is, is an attempt to lighten the mood. We are bored out of our skulls, and what better way than to lighten the mood than with a tarot reading? What is the worst it can be? The Death card? Please.

Of course, it backfires immediately.

Nia pulls three cards for the group of us.

There is The Fool.

"That's you." Priya whispers loudly to Nia. "You're the fool."

"Uh huh."

I'm trying not to smile. Nia pulls the second card, the Eight of Swords. A woman bound and blindfolded, set against a stage of eight upright swords.

"And that one's you?" Nia asks.

"I mean, it can if you want it to be. You wanna tie me down, all you gotta do is ask."

"Can you two horndogs shut up? Your flirting is making me nauseous."

Nia flips the third and final card:

Six of Swords.

Swords are the suit of higher consciousness, change, and power. Major Arcana—face cards—are so often what's shown in movies and books. It's easier for querents to parse out what it means when you see a crash of lightning rupture a Tower to rubble than to interpret the meaning behind a ship, a ferryman shepherding two passengers, cutting a deep bog toward a distant land. Are these waters the Slough of Despond? Is it a passage fraught with danger? Is that island a safe harbour when the winds blow? And what do the swords have to do with any of that?

Tarot is often so obscured, I think, interpreted through the paintbrush strokes of memory and fantasy. Wants, desires, fears. What I can imagine for myself could mean something completely other to Priya and Nia.

I look at Priya. I don't know why I'm so fixed on her. Maybe because it feels made for her. Maybe because I've taken her meds and I feel bad. Maybe, maybe, maybe.

"Where do you see yourself in the cards?" Nia asks her.

There is a stunned silence.

I am expecting Priya to point to the bound woman, trapped, or even the fool, ironically tripping off a cliff, but no. Instead, Priya points to the third card.

The woman—

Hesitates.

The child—

Finally landing on the cloaked figure.

The ferryman.

That makes sense. Priya does seem to me like the type who feels comfortable in charge, a captain with confidence, active in steering to a better end. But what of the ferryman who is also just a passenger?

Maybe the journey to this new terrain feels unfamiliar, a movement towards a shore in which men kill each other on purpose. It's one thing to view it from a safe distance, on television, in the news. But to be in it . . . moving towards it . . .

There is a hope, a belief, a faith, that maybe the destination will be better than the familiar terrain of anxiety from which we've now just departed.

Sometimes the new world we face is more terrifying than we could have ever imagined. Further, we aren't just visitors, blessed with the boon of return, but soon to be inhabitants. Grief and sadness may exist in the land of the innocent, but in the land of the seasoned, fear and wrath dominate all, and the ferryman can but paddle through.

I'm not sure when *they*, the people in the image, became *we*, but there it is. I suppose I see myself in this after all. When things look good, I tell myself tarot will divine the future. When things look bad, I like to tell myself tarot means nothing. Simply a path given if no change is made.

I once pulled this card for Priya, and it heralded the start of her new relationship with Nia.

How different the card looks to me now. It is portentous, and yet, there is a stillness in knowing of an inevitable journey forward, where truths will finally be revealed. Are we ready to hear such truths?

Should I tell Priya what I've done? I, of course, want the shore to be better from the ones from which we've come, but there is no guarantee of that. And I haven't even looked at the other two cards. The truth is, I have no easy answers.

I want to cheerfully blurt: *we're going through a transition, from rough waters to smooth sailing up ahead*, I want to be the ferryman of this situation, and shepherd these lost souls with compassion to a place of hope. But I can't guarantee that, especially after what I've done. All I can do is steer us through the cards, from familiar anxieties to a new shore, to consider what might be implied by a pull like this. It is a grave responsibility, and this wasn't even my suggestion to begin with. I don't know what lies in wait on the other side, or how prepared we really are to meet it. All I know is:

There's no going back.

After last night's tarot reading, Priya complains of a searing heat and visual hallucinations—the ground writhing, *alive*. I've likened it to the onset of panic and emesis. When I tell her to eat, despite her lack of appetite, I notice something flicker in her eyes. A lack of recognition. A sheen. Something not quite right. Here is the lotus of it, blooming to fruition. And with it, here it comes. My final adjuration. Sitting at my desk, editing a scene on my laptop, Priya checks my bedroom door open. It slams open against the side of the dresser, which leaves a dent in the door's face. Priya is yelling at me before I can even register that she's here.

On her phone is the single post announcing my short film at the Toronto After Dark film festival.

Her words, at first low and questioning, slowly transition to a spilling black cloud of vitriol as she realizes what it is that I've done.

"You spineless bitch—you went behind my back?"

No feigning. There goes my little magpie nest of lies, swept off in a storm. She's sticking the phone in my face, teaser trailer of my short film auto-playing. Clips of Priya—camera light scorching her face, keening audio that seems to warp her flesh. A horrible little worm mouth against my abdomen. Priya. Beautiful Priya, her eyes past the horizon of many seasons, hair falling like gentle petals on the liquid of her skin. And her body doing that unnatural thing.

I can't look at her. Her voice, agony edged with hysteria.

"You took my shit? You took my shit, and you filmed me?"

"It's not like I published your fucking diary."

I don't know how this is helping. It's not. Her face twists into a pale mask of rage. She looks sick, a storm tower claimed by the elements.

It's like everything else that's just happened flies out the window.

"You didn't even want it—look what it's doing to you!"

"You're a fucking animal, you know that? You take and you take. You didn't want me to submit to After Dark just so you could?"

I bleat out a harsh laugh. "That's fucking rich, coming from you. You take just as much! You couldn't let me have this one thing!"

"No, *you* couldn't let *me* have this one thing. You take everything! I was trying to find a sense of belonging. I took the story down—I took it down for you."

"It was just a tweet."

She shakes her head no. "It wasn't. It's all this and more."

"What the hell do you mean, 'all this'?"

"For someone who wants to be seen as such an intellectual, you're really dumb sometimes, you know that? This isn't some Ottessa Moshfegh wet dream of yours. Wake up. You're so fucking disconnected from reality you can't even differentiate between issues you make up in your head and issues going on in real life."

I scoff. "Like what?"

"The biggest issue you have is with people misgendering you when you are a straight-passing, cis-passing, fem-presenting tenderqueer."

"Those are called microaggressions and they're valid."

"Yes, they are. They absolutely are. But it's not helpful for you to focus on those little things and use them to justify having zero coping mechanisms or helping other people out with the privileges you've been given."

"I help you out all the time."

"Do you? Do you, Luca? 'Cause I sure as hell don't fucking see it. All I see is a capitalist and a parasite. Someone who takes and takes. It must be exhausting to be you. You're so neurotic, you compare yourself against everything!"

I don't say anything.

"Why? Why would you even do that?"

The hurt in her voice flares a red in me. A deep, red pit that feels so big I don't think I can stop what's coming next.

She shakes her head, exasperated. "If you took two fucking seconds to stop googling your own name and look around you—"

"The film doesn't belong to you. I have the right to—"

"The *right*? I have the right not to be used!"

"You can barely even see your face."

"What am I supposed to be—thankful for that?" She stares at me a moment, assessing. "Jealous, is that it?"

"That makes zero fucking sense."

"Oh yeah, it does. You can't stand the thought that I'd make it big without you. That I might've made something ten times as successful, that I might garner some glimpse of something from my lived experience that you could never—"

"That is a *lie*."

"You love to omit the fact that you come from a wealthy family, that your fancy private school and your daddy paying for all the digi equipment and the apps and the workshops, even your share of this apartment—that even after all of that, you can't fathom the fact that someone with *none* of that might not only make it further than you with the same nugget of inspiration, but that they might overtake you. That the hardest part of your fucking day, might be accidentally over-tipping a barista when you're buying an oat milk matcha latte or whatever the fuck it is that fuels you these days."

Tears in my eyes then. Brimming and full of hate and wanting to hit her. Dimming my accomplishments, diminishing them to the dark star of nepotism. Heat rising and gathering in my face, down my limbs like an electric rush into my hands, balled into fists.

Rotten taste in my mouth.

Priya, so calm, cool, collected. Not even mad anymore, just disappointed. Superiority complex, looking down on me, shit-on-her-shoe stare that she garnered from Robin—oh, how we imprint these things on each other—and I can't take that look on her face. I can't fucking take it.

"I'm not going to fight you," she says. "But I won't stand by as you take everything—"

"Oh, you're above arguing. You're so different from everyone else."

"You want to hit me?"

"Fuck you. You're dead to me."

Big fucking deal, her face seems to say.

"You're so fucking unbelievable," Priya says. "You make everything about you. You want a fucking fight? You wanna be about that life? Well, here—"

I feel it gather like a coming storm. Rising in us. *Let it happen*, I think. *Let it happen.*

And it does. It does.

Priya punches me. Right in the stomach. I flinch my eyes closed and step back instinctively to absorb the blow, but it's almost like there's no natural physics applying here. Her fist mushes in like a rotten pumpkin, sucking at her wrist, and then deeper.

My eyes open now. Open wide as though waking to a nightmare, and from this place screaming, my body reeling in some brutal need to have her, what she is or has, potential written into the wiry frame of her body; cutting myself wide open for it so I can fit it in. And Priya, screaming, stop it, stop it, *LUCA, STOP IT*, both of us falling back, her onto me, into me, grabbing my arm. Sudden smell like rotted fruit. Like shit. Like blood, thick and hot against my hands. Priya's fingers corseting my throat, all her strength pulling away, but me, my rage stronger, like a Chinese finger trap, choking her down now, forcing her into my own body like a snake. I don't know where she's going—I'm not swelling, not gestating like a pregnancy, but still that hole in me is swallowing her down. Up her elbow and to her shoulder, where her bone breaks, contorts at a disfigured angle—

And Priya *screams*. Inhuman sound. Sound I never knew she, or anyone, could make, animalistic and heavy with grief. I try to shove her off, but instead of the resistance of flesh beneath her shirt, there is a softness that yields and tugs at my fingers that makes me yelp. My fist jerks back like a loaded spring. When she tries to retract her arm and do the same, my navel tears away the gelatinous skin off her bone like the rind off a fruit with a sickening *pop!* and what's underneath glistens coral and blood-rust red.

The lines between us begin to collapse. Not once does my body pause or falter.

We are like two coins on a train track flattened into one. One of us was always going to win out. There could be no collaboration. There is no mutual aid in times of war. I have to collapse her and have what's left. I have to reduce her to silt and sediment, carried by the channels of my veins into the harbour of my body, no longer particularized. Her screams are drenched in terror, her blood running down my sides and soaking into the carpet. The petrified statue of her cracks and lets something out, a scintillating iridescence. Across my body's edifice, the veins and organs crawl out from inside her, mesh together in a latticework membrane against my own, bursting out of her and reaching, melding, together with mine.

I can't help but choke out a laugh. It dribbles out, thin and demented.

I can't tell what it is that I've stolen, only that I took something, and a bite out of Priya's arm. I can hear her shriek; that terrible sound. I'm scared to look, but I follow it with my eye, down, down, where my shirt has pulled up from our fall and there on my belly: the hungry little hole, mouth open, sightless baby bird—say *ahh*— gorging itself without teeth, dissolving Priya into some guttural pocket dimension—empty, save for acid and vitriol, no room for anything else, only that endless hunger that might just be glutted by the meal of obliterating the one person—the one friend—who might have stuck with me through it all, 'til the end. I can't bear the thought, but it's almost like this thing is more powerful than me, has been festering for so much longer, unfed, because the screaming has stopped and when I open my eyes, for the first time in what feels like an endless series of gestures, I am unable to move.

Priya is reduced to a swampy, crimson stain on the carpet. Her head is intact, but where the mouth in my stomach punched through, her face isn't. Like an anvil on a water balloon. Her face is stripped of flesh, split entirely open like ripened fruit.

I can finally see the hole on her abdomen. It is like mine, but undersized, malnourished. Starved.

The force of internal trauma against the main cavity of her body has caused a thick, dark smear to blow out her anus. It extends a fifth of the room, and I'm staring at it incomprehensibly for a moment before I realize it is entrails.

Worse, she is still alive. Gurgling some strangled incantation.

I recoil before collecting myself and futilely scampering back a pace.

Her arm extends, searching, finds the edge of my ankle and clamps gently on the cuff of my shin. She emits a thin wail, like a dying animal.

I try to pull away, thinking about Winnie, my childhood cat that got hit by a car. How I saw her on my street, her innards pulped to a paste, and wanted so badly to keep her chunky paws, preserve the little stumps with taxidermy.

"It's okay," I say, trying to keep the shaking from my voice. "Priya, it's going to be okay. You're going to be okay." My timbre is full of shame. And Christ, I am scared. I look down at my stomach, usually flat, but blackened with blood. When I think I see a face there, clouded in blind hunger, I clench my eyes shut. Look over. Choose to see instead the spattered corpse of a woman still dying in my arms. I don't want to look at the face of what made me do this. My sanity is already skating along the eroding surface of icy waters, and I don't want to peer down, too afraid to drown. Don't think I can take it.

It gives me nightmares for weeks. In them, I dream of Priya, of my body moving of its own accord; I dream of the eyes of a face which would drive someone to this, and it is my face; dreams of a massive black maw opening up before me, within me. Dreams of worshippers draping their skin over my bloodied body, dreams of them embedding themselves into me. In them, the sky smoulders, darkening to a dusk-grey.

X

While I gather myself, they plan a funeral for the calcified shell of Priya, or what's left of her, anyway. I don't go. Maybe that is cowardly of me, but Priya was the glue holding our friend group together, and I don't think anyone—especially Nia—would stand to see me there. Besides, even without going, I see her in my dreams. I think half my life is lived in dreams now. In them, we kneel over Priya's empty coffin. Robin smokes a whole joint to herself and holds Nia when, inevitably, she begins to cry. I ask Nia's forgiveness and she says nothing—does not even give me the pity of words. She merely stares, her gaze burning into me like cigarette stubs.

I get checked into the clinic for anomalies—dewdrop spores of tumor growths, threatening to grow bloated and putrefying—which eventually fade, though the reek of cauterized flesh stains my clothes.

This thing whittles me away, all while I go through court lawsuits that last eighteen months. One with Priya's family for criminal charges, one with the research unit responsible for our clinical trial. No winning that. Absolutely no winning against Big Pharma. But, hey, little things. My name is plastered everywhere like a divine doctrine. People know it. Know my name, know my work. A religion, sure. Viral things can do that. Virus, parasite, god. Primitive instinct of moving towards the masses. Superficial, sacrificial, Priya at the altar and me with athame blade in hand, skin slick with blood. How much blood? How much and for what?

My short film is pulled from the festival and gets used as evidence in the trial. It's leaked, and a subculture forms out of the video of Priya sleepwalking, and then I get paid by tabloid journalists for more footage—any clips related to the trial—and I lose every penny to the lawyers. The world is an endless shrill of questions and commands. In the end, I am sentenced to nothing. The jury does not convict. How could they? It's not like I did it on purpose.

When I think about it, one of our bodies had to win out. Mine, I suppose. The advantage of money and education and all that.

What's the matter? Isn't this exactly what you wanted? Dollar signs in your eyes. Fingers in every pie, you got your name on everything from Mediterranean to Boardwalk Avenue. She's gone and you're famous. Got everything you wanted, right?

That's rich.

Priya. Her voice, not mine.

She is speaking without speaking.

Every day that it shifts, it shifts us closer together and further apart. Her voice inside me quiets, until I can no longer hear it.

And I hate myself for it. I'd rather shit glass than abandon Priya, but I was a reckless coward, and here I am, trapped in a liminal coffin pulsing down the throat of eternity, the shiny veneer of my name pasted across every newspaper and magazine, and for what? For what?

Sometimes I still dream of her. In the dreams, I'm hiding in a locked bathroom, Priya's freckle-smattered hand up my leg, dragging her fingers across my back, mapping the topography of my body. The last footage that I have of Priya is that stupid digicam recording, and it's forever been interwoven with clips of my own body going awry. I can't even watch it anymore. It's just a reminder, an archive of what we were, what I did, that she was my closest friend. Keeping a record of time in two ways. What are people but facsimiles of moments? Even if it disappears, it is on film. There is proof. There is proof in two places—three, if you count the palace of the mind—where we were friends 'til that betrayal.

Two weeks later and the final cheque for the trial itself comes. A measly six-hundred bucks. Just enough to buy Priya a plane ticket to San Francisco for her Helix filmmaking workshop. Six hundred bucks that is nothing to me. Six hundred bucks that I easily piss away on Ubers and takeout and Patreon memberships I don't even check. I sit alone in my room with my bank cheque and stare down at it.

Was it worth it?

My throat clenches shut.

The cheque drops from my hands. Outside, the street blackens, and there are no more songs or tarot readings or braided hair or petals of skin. It's all so exquisitely sad. I sit here, alone, and I feel like a god. A lonely Monotheistic god.

YOUR NEXT BEST AMERICAN GIRL

NADIA BULKIN

1. THE WOMAN BEHIND THE MASK

VERONICA LEANED TOWARD the full-length mirror to check on the status of the blackheads on her nose; leaving the salicylic acid on overnight was definitely helping dissolve them. Then she turned to eyeball the thickness of her body's profile—she was doing a juice cleanse in the hopes of not needing to suck in her stomach so hard at Miss Pioneer Spirit this weekend—but before she could roll her gaze down to her stomach, it snagged on something else. Something far more alarming.

Three round red sores on her right arm, each about an inch wide, snuggled so close together that they almost looked like the bite of a three-fanged monster. Or a crimson set of insect eyes.

She stared at them for so long that they started to stare back at her.

She touched one of the sores with a cringe, hoping it wouldn't be wet. And it wasn't—it was worse. Half-gummy, half-crusted. Like something that had been left inside an oven for too long. Completely disgusting.

The bed, she thought. Something had bit her in bed. Veronica grabbed her jumble of bedsheets, wondering if she had the will to smash a poodle-sized spider, but when she tore the sheets away there was nothing—no sign of any animal incursion, and when she scanned the rest of her body, no other sores, either.

Her mother Irene cringed when she showed her. And then, as Irene was wont to do, she immediately turned away and decided it wasn't her problem.

"I bet it's because you're so busy," Irene said. "Stress is bad for the skin, you know."

Sometimes Veronica wondered if she'd be happier living in the campus dorms, bonding with girls who knew nothing about pageants over froyo and pizza. She could almost imagine herself, sometimes, as a normal twenty-one-year-old. But every dollar they saved on room and board costs went straight back into financing her dream of being crowned Miss Americana. First, the entry fees for the local preliminaries—she couldn't assume she'd win the first one she entered, so that line item needed extra. Second, the entry fee for Miss Heartland Americana—fingers crossed that she made it that far. Third, wardrobe. Fourth, beauty supplies and treatments. Fifth, hotel and gas. Not everybody had a suburban megachurch to sponsor them like Addison Dove. Some people had to make sacrifices.

"You know what you need?" Irene said. "To *relax*. Take another one of your steam baths."

That was not, in fact, what she needed. Miss Pioneer Spirit was in four days. She needed to not look like she was growing *berries* out of her arm.

She took the grossest pictures of the sores she could and texted them to Dr. Gillies. *Need these gone by Saturday!!!* Three exclamation marks because it had taken her three weeks of begging to get him to approve chemical peels for her acne scars, a routine treatment that every other girl competing for Miss Americana was undoubtedly getting monthly. She'd probably be relegated to the Ms. division before he approved baby Botox for her forehead.

Then she headed to campus, putting on the latest episode of the *Pageant World* podcast hosted by former Miss Americana and current pageant coach Tanya O'Dell. The episode was called "Five Mindset Hacks to Win Your Next Pageant," and she willed it to be a positive omen for this weekend's contest. You couldn't punch your ticket to Miss Heartland Americana by winning Miss Pioneer Spirit—you could get a ton of other prizes, though, courtesy of its big ag sponsors—but you could see how much you needed to panic. A good showing at Miss Pioneer Spirit meant your outfits were good and your talent routine was solid, and you'd probably snatch a ticket by winning one of the early local preliminaries. A bad showing at Miss Pioneer Spirit meant you had less than two weeks to re-sculpt yourself into the form of a queen.

"The first hack is: don't let fear rule your heart. It's okay to be nervous! But don't make decisions because you're scared. The girls that play it safe? They might place in the top ten. But they'll never win. Because nobody will remember them."

Dr. Gillies phoned in a prescription for a steroid cream by lunchtime, promising the redness would go down "immediately."

But when she ripped the bag open in the convenience store parking lot and lathered the cream on her arm's unholy trifecta, the only thing she felt was a sizzling, stinging pain.

"The pain means it's working," she muttered, curling her toes into the soles of her shoes and through those shoes into the carpet floor of her car. "The pain means it's going away."

Backstage at Miss Pioneer Spirit, a pretty blonde in a magenta power suit was talking to Addison, making big cartoonish gestures with her long pink nails. Last year's Miss Heartland Americana, Jenna Bublik. She'd gotten tanner, and fillers, since she won the title.

Veronica and Nayeli squinted at what looked from a distance like a game of charades, trying to interpret the advice that Addison's parents had paid Jenna to give their daughter. Was it—tilt your chin up really high? Widen your eyes so the judges could see the whites all the way around? Make werewolf claws out of your hands? Act demon-possessed? Whatever it was, Addison was nodding thoughtfully.

"Maybe she's saying to growl at the judges," Veronica suggested. "*Grrrrr.*"

Nayeli chuckled at first, but then her voice dropped and she muttered, "Hey, Jenna would know."

Veronica glanced at her best friend. Nayeli was picking at the fringes dangling from her red-white-and-blue dress, a somewhat desperate attempt to cater to Miss Pioneer Spirit's all-American theme. Veronica thought she'd probably crossed the line into kitsch, given she was also playing "America the Beautiful" on the violin, but Nayeli's sister said she had to "compensate" here in the heartland. "Gotta keep up with all the gringas," as she put it, staring meaningfully at blonde Veronica.

"Whatever," she said, trying to lighten the mood, "Jenna wasn't even top ten at Miss Americana anyway."

"Ooh, I'm *Veronica*, I don't need *Jenna* because I have *Lucrece.*"

Veronica rolled her eyes while a small smile crept onto her lips. Not too big a smile, though, because while Lucrece had placed second runner-up at Miss Americana, it had been twenty years ago. In those days, Miss Americana had been about composure and restraint and grace like a diamond under pressure—and when it came to evening gown, Lucrece's sense of posture was still undefeated. She knew how to exude the glamour of an art deco silhouette, the precise shape of a perfume bottle. It was why they got along so well, she and Lucrece. They shared an understanding of beauty.

But sometimes Veronica did worry that Lucrece was too conservative. She didn't think girls ought to be getting plastic surgery. She was skeptical of the freelance photographers who hung around pageants, offering to add photos to girls' portfolios. She didn't follow any start-up hair and makeup brands that were always looking for brand ambassadors. She understood that Lucrece had had some bad experiences in the aftermath of her Miss Americana run—she hadn't shared details, but Veronica assumed it involved one or more creepy men—but she also didn't want to let fear rule her heart, as Tanya O'Dell said.

"I bet she's saying," Veronica said, nestling what was thankfully her unblemished arm against Nayeli's shoulder, "to not let fear rule your heart."

"Aww . . ." Nayeli rolled her eyes. "Dork."

"Just one final question, Veronica—how'd you get that bandage on your arm?"

The sores on her right arm had not gone away in the intervening four days. In fact, Dr. Gillies' treatment only seemed to make them angrier, redder, more horrifically bulbous than they already were. One in-person visit and two telehealth appointments had not helped clarify the crisis. "Give it time," he said at first, and then, "We don't want to make them more irritated." Like they were in a hostage situation, and he was too much of a coward to go in guns blazing.

All of which meant that Veronica had been forced to drive around the city yesterday, buying every type of adhesive bandage she could find. FlexStretch and HydroSafe and PermaStay and the like. "What about this one? Can you see this one?" she'd repeatedly asked Irene, who'd glance up from her phone, squint at Veronica's tricep, and say, "Well, yes . . ." She thought she'd picked the one that would look the least obtrusive against her skin. Evidently, she had failed.

"Um . . . " Under the stage lights, Veronica's mind flitted like a housefly from one outdoor activity to another—a world of mud and gasoline that she had never known, but had overheard boys and girls chatter about during passing periods at Wanahoo High. She needed something that would balance out her clean-cut, paper doll image. Something that would appeal to the downhome country judges of Miss Pioneer Spirit. One of them, the wife of the Forger Foods CEO, blinked her long eyelashes in exaggerated expectation.

"I was riding an ATV through the woods and scraped my arm against some bushes," Veronica said, forcing a ghostly giggle. "Sometimes I can be a bit clumsy."

The judges chuckled. Mrs. Forger Foods CEO raised her painted eyebrows. At least they couldn't knock her for being over-rehearsed this time.

Addison was just behind the stage, having the last tresses of her chestnut hair delicately curled by her mother. As Veronica passed them, trying not to trip over the taped-down electrical cables, Addison gave her a smile so fake it would have curdled milk. "I didn't know you rode ATVs, Dairy Queen," she purred. "That's *cool*." Addison's mother giggled, "Addy, don't be mean."

Obviously, it wasn't cool. And obviously, Addison's mother wanted her to be mean. Addison's mother had probably given the bitch the idea to put glue on Veronica's headband at Junior Miss Bliss a few years ago. It was insane that Addison hadn't been banned from every pageant in the region after that. She "didn't know the glue was so strong," apparently. What a joke. But then, pageantry was just a twisted simulacrum of real life. The harshest sort of light, the kind that burned away comforting lies like "high school isn't forever" and "sooner or later, everyone grows up."

It was then, after Addison's snide comment, that the itching started. No, itching was too gentle of a word for the eruption on her arm. More like a pulsing. A pounding. By the time the judges were ready to announce the winners and all the contestants teetered back up on stage, Veronica had to grind her teeth together to push the desire to scratch her arm bloody to the back aisles of her consciousness.

Stephanie Agar won Miss Congeniality. Jada Poppy won Miss Photogenic. Krista Spoot won Second Runner-Up. Excitement at the possibility of an improbable victory temporarily overtook the itch and she glanced across the stage, hoping to exchange an encouraging smile with Nayeli. But it was Addison who she caught looking at her, eyes narrow with scorn. It only lasted a second before Addison swiveled her head away and gave the audience a big lupine grin.

"Our first runner-up . . . "

Not me, not me, not me

"Contestant number eleven, Veronica Muenster!"

Damn. But Lucrece had trained her for these moments, and Veronica swallowed the disappointment so fast it gave her heartburn. She clamped on her perfectly-calibrated gracious loser smile, accepted the little plastic trophy as if it was a presidential medal of honor, and golf-clapped when Addison was announced as the winner. Again.

But at some point during the ritual of crowning—maybe it was when the sash slipped over Addison's shoulder?—her dam of control broke. In one swift fall from grace, Veronica passed the award to her right hand so she could claw her left into the latex covering her sores and *dig*. Dig deep into that cluster of *wrong* just begging to be corrected. She imagined her fingernails scraping muscle, grazing bone, ripping tendons open and apart. Imagined her fingers pushing past all the damaged tissue, all the way through to the other side of her arm where the air and her skin would be clean and free. What a dream.

The pain that radiated from her arm was so satisfying—like a firm pluck of her most sensitive nerve endings—that she actually let out a small noise, of obscenity and delight.

Veronica and Nayeli pried off their tippy-top heels on their way back to the dressing room, groaning as the plastic separated from their swollen, contorted feet. Veronica had expected her arm to be bleeding from all the scratching she'd done on stage, but her fingernails had only collected a gory red crust. Nayeli's eyes were black with mascara smudge, victims of her bad habit of wiping when she felt tears coming on.

"You'd think they would like patriotic Latina bullshit," Nayeli huffed. She was referring to Winnie Hu, last year's Miss West Coast Americana who'd done a baton twirling routine in a stars and stripes mini dress. "I guess that's only good for *some* brown people."

Some girl they barely knew was crying in the corner of the dressing room, but otherwise, they were alone. While Nayeli went to tear herself out of her dress, Veronica glanced at the area that had been Addison's station. One of her monogrammed tote bags had been left, mouth open, in the chair she'd been sitting in. Veronica glanced over her shoulder to check that Nayeli still had her back turned. What did the police always say when they confiscated stuff without a warrant? That it was lying in "plain sight?" Veronica snuck up on the bag and peeked in.

There was body spray (Eternal Joy, whatever that smelled like). Painkillers (extra strength). Bronzer (Jenna's idea, probably). And one pale blue tube that looked oddly, horribly familiar. Everything that Veronica got specially formulated from Dr. Gillies was branded like that—had Addison somehow *stolen* her moisturizer? In a white-hot state of incredulous rage, she reached into the bag and grabbed it.

"Vee," Nayeli called. "Are you done changing?"

It was indeed from Dr. Gillies. But it was prescribed for Addison. There were ingredients on there that she recognized from her own supposedly secret formula, high-value ingredients that she'd paid a premium for—if, in fact, she was actually getting any of those ingredients. She hadn't seen any sores sprouting on Addison's perfectly sun-kissed skin, after all. Of course, no one would dare shaft the great Addison Dove, already an ambassador to five brands. But Veronica the Dairy Queen, sponsor of none? A cheap knock-off would do. Just mix some petroleum jelly with some parabens and call it a fucking day.

A furious roar arose from her right arm and she sank three of her nails, still coated with a paste of bloody dead skin cells, into the bandage. She was trying to push each nail into a sore, as if preparing to rip off her arm and throw it down a bowling lane.

"Are you snooping?" Nayeli asked, suddenly digging her chin into Veronica's shoulder and prying at the fingers holding the moisturizer. "What is that?"

"Nothing." Veronica threw the bottle back into the bag. "Some crap."

She waited until she was in the car to pry off the bandage and check the damage she'd done to herself. Her fears were confirmed when she saw *five* little sores bubbling away in the heat of the bandage, not *three*. Two more tiny lakes of fire. Two more little uprisings. And then she jolted forward, the seatbelt hitting her throat, as Irene hit the brake. "Oh God," Irene was saying, "now what's that guy doing?"

A disheveled-looking man in an ill-fitting suit was standing in the middle of the parking lot with a bullhorn, steadfastly ignoring everyone else's nasty looks. "Little children, keep yourselves from idols!" he was yelling, "Get on your knees and repent, you women of Zion! Beg for forgiveness for your vanity!"

When Addison emerged from the convention center at the nucleus of a lively human swarm, the protesting man picked up his heels and started weaving between cars to get closer to her. As if he was called, moth-like, by her sun-sparkling crown. He wasn't moving very fast, and every step he took was met by vigorous minivan honking, but he still carried with him a vague sense of threat, an urgency that seemed combustible, unstable.

"Miss, you take that crown off your head!" he commanded Addison, one hand outstretched and pointing at her scalp as if he meant to rip it off himself. Addison froze. Her mother screamed. The protesting man was ten feet away from them, now. "That crown is not yours! Give it back to our Almighty God or risk eternal damnation!"

A man in a fleece pullover who Veronica remembered to be Addison's dad went barreling up to the protesting man, his face contorted purple in anger, and punched him in the head. Veronica couldn't quite tell what Addison's father was saying, after the protesting man fell on his ass and just lay there—*sick freak*, maybe.

"I hope you don't expect me to start beating people up for you," Irene muttered as she took her foot off the brake, "if you ever start collecting fans like that."

Over the next week, Veronica tried to put the fact that Dr. Gillies was also Addison's doctor out of her mind. She had to fill out her entry forms for Miss Summerall—the first and most prestigious Miss Heartland Americana preliminary, and one that Addison was more likely than not to win, given how decisively she'd won Miss Pioneer Spirit.

Lucrece would have smacked her on the hand if she'd heard her say that. "There are no done deals," Lucrece would say, "What do they say in sport? You have to play the game."

A notification on her phone drew her away from the question of why she should win Miss Summerall: Miss Pioneer Spirit had tagged her in two photos. One was a group shot with all the contestants—her eye went straight to beaming Addison with her five-inch princess tiara in the center of the stage—and the other was a solo shot of her receiving her runner-up trophy. Thankfully, it was taken before her little itching incident.

Veronica zoomed in on her face and opened her notebook. Her eyes looked especially asymmetrical in the photo—could eyeliner compensate for that? Better brow threading? It was a poor angle on her nose. And her teeth needed another round of whitening. When she first started pageantry at age twelve, it would have killed her to write so harshly about herself. Now it was an addiction. Because every flaw she could dissect now was a possible future point in her favor.

Lucrece had taught her that: control every point you can. Veronica knew she was no great beauty. "Weirdo," they called her in school, because her eyes were disproportionately large and her sense of fashion was about five decades out-of-date and she never understood their jokes. But Lucrece had shown her that a billion little tweaks could transform a sparrow into a swan.

And then there was the bandage. She zoomed in on that, too. Was there a bit of red peeking through? The sores seemed to be pushing against the latex, just enough to cast the smallest of lumpy shadows. God—they made her want to vomit. She zoomed back out in a useless attempt to get away from them, and noticed two new comments on the photo.

This girl is such a crown-chaser lol, the first comment read. *Kinda sad.*

Never gonna happen, read the second. *#TeamAddison*

An unholy itch rose out of her arm again. She was wearing a tank top to try to give it air, but air wasn't helping much. She slapped her hand against the itch to try to numb the fire—only to realize that she was pawing at the wrong arm. Her left arm. With her heart plunging up into her throat, Veronica twisted toward the mirror.

More sores. Her left arm, this time. For a second she thought she'd gone crazy, until she realized that these holes were farther down her arm than the first set. She stepped in front of her full-length mirror and rotated both arms forward. Hunching. Yes, two clusters. Both sides now.

As if he'd been summoned, her phone dinged with a text from Dr. Gillies. *Hi Veronica*, it read, *how's the arm doing?*

Was he mocking her? How much was Addison's family paying him?

How much poison might have seeped into her skin since she first met him?

Every tube, every jar, every bottle filled with serum—none of it could ever touch her skin again. She raced downstairs to grab one of the large black kitchen garbage bags and a pair of cleaning gloves, then back upstairs to throw each container into an impromptu quarantine. She really belted them, too. The better to get the rage out, since she would never be able to go to Dr. Gillies' office and throw them in his face, see how he liked *growths* coming out of his cheeks—could she? No. It would be beyond disqualifying. They had disqualified Samara Farro from Miss New England Americana for posting a "fuck you" sticker on her school's social feed.

"Oh my . . . " Irene had followed her upstairs and now poked her head in the doorway. "What on Earth are you doing?"

"We need to find a new dermatologist," Veronica said. "I want a second opinion."

2. THE WOMAN AND THE SECRET

Her second opinion, from a dermatologist whose website promised a full arsenal of state-of-the-art technology to support his patients' skin care goals, was as bad as the first. In fact, it was worse. "Have you heard of dermatillomania?" he asked.

Veronica shook her head, but she didn't like the sound of that "mania." Her skin felt manic, all right, but didn't doctors only use mania to describe what happened in people's heads?

"It's an obsessive skin-picking disease."

Veronica narrowed her eyes. "I don't pick my skin."

Even though she had a roaring hunger, just then, to run her fingers over her face and feel for new bumps, ridges, indentations. Her left hand, the one that had served as an agent of her disgrace at Miss Pioneer Spirit, twitched with a desire that she immediately and tightly clasped. No. She did not pick her skin.

Dr. McIndoe pursed his lips together, barely trying to hold back his skepticism. "Do you think there's any chance you're doing it in your sleep?"

Incredulous, Veronica held up her hands—the hands that she took painstaking care not to pick at, not to dehydrate, not to even *use* if she'd had a fresh manicure. "Wouldn't my nails be all bloody if I was doing that?"

Because he apparently didn't have a comeback to that, Dr. McIndoe turned to Irene. "Mom," he said, as if she was his mother, as if it was her name, "What do you think?"

"Well." Irene took a deep inhale, bending back to scrutinize Veronica from an angle, the way she'd squint at a sloppily-assembled holiday window display. "I mean, I don't have eyes on her all the time. But there was that little . . . " Irene did a jazz hands shake, " . . . *episode* you had during Miss Pioneer Spirit . . . "

Instantly, her entire carpet of skin began to tingle. "It was itchy from the bandage!"

Irene looked plaintively at Dr. McIndoe. He was her type, Veronica thought. A silver-tongued, silver-haired charmer who knew how to lean theatrically against the counter as if auditioning for the role of "handsome doctor" on a daytime soap. "She just went to *town* on those sores on her right arm. It was terrible."

Goddamn Irene. Veronica could see Dr. McIndoe nodding sympathetically, firming up his opinion, so she had to jump in: "No, no—okay, fine—I scratched it that *one time,* and I agree, I shouldn't have, it only made it worse." Even if it had felt so good. "But doctor, I promise you, I woke up with these . . . whatever these are, these wounds. In fact, I have reason to believe . . . " she took a deep, centering breath. "I have reason to believe that I may have been poisoned."

"I understand your concern," Dr. McIndoe claimed, falsely, "but the thing is, Veronica, I don't see any sign of toxin or any sign of any environmental contaminant whatsoever."

She didn't know how that was relevant—didn't toxins wash out? Wasn't he supposed to be a doctor? "Did you look at the bottles I brought you?" She could see him breathing in, preparing an answer that she could already tell would not inspire confidence. "Like, *really* look at them, send them to a lab to do a full chemical analysis and everything?"

"I've reviewed the ingredient list," he said. "And there's nothing unusual about the formula. It's almost exactly what I would have prescribed myself."

For a moment Veronica imagined a great gathering of dermatologist mercenaries, Dr. Gillies and Dr. McIndoe included, looming over a list of pageant contestants who had or had not paid them off. Imagined them crossing out her name. "I'm not asking you about what it says on the stickers that are printed on the side. I'm asking you about what they actually contain."

For a few minutes they stared at each other, she and the dermatologist. "I'll send them to a lab," he said at last, "but only if you promise to start wearing gloves at night."

On the eve of Miss Summerall, Veronica lay on her bed and fantasized about cauterizing her skin. Putting a heated knife to those awful little colonies on her arms and burning them alive, Old Testament-style. "The Wrath of God," she'd call it.

She was supposed to be relaxing, the better to whittle away her supposed demonic inner urge to scratch away her skin. Irene was far too enthusiastic about the treatment plan—lighting her a lavender candle, making her chamomile tea, helping her slide on her dermatillomania gloves—it was the most mothering she'd done in years. "Now don't you take it off before your alarm goes off tomorrow morning," Irene said, wagging her finger. "Promise me."

It made Veronica wonder if she was the butt of a universal joke.

Just inside the open closet door was the peach sleeveless gown that she'd hoped to wear at Miss Summerall. That plan, like the skin around her sores, was dead. Her sores were too many, by now, to cover up with bandages. Her limbs looked like stony coral, pale landscapes riddled with tiny red hills that were too many to count – she'd given up a few days ago – but almost lovely in their natural symmetry. Almost.

Lucrece thought she should go without bandages and just show her skin, "warts and all!", but Veronica assumed she was drunk. There was no loveliness in her scabies-limbs. Instead, she was wearing a long-sleeved navy dress that she'd bought when Felicity Nigella went viral for competing in a full coverage velour gown a few years back. Of course, that gown had matched Felicity's platform—it was a statement about the risk posed by Earth's increasingly extreme weather, or something. She wondered where Felicity was now. Chained to a tree or throwing blood at a government official, probably.

Maybe she could change her platform to awareness of dermatological disaster. The oversexualization of women's arms.

And hope that the navy dress's hip-high slit and the six-inch silver heels she'd be wearing would make up for the lack of skin up top.

Lack of skin. She would love to not have skin. Just a smooth expanse of muscle, strong and stretchy and streamlined. Shining bloody crimson beneath the lights, in perfect contrast to a white dress. And completely devoid of scabs. Because it wasn't even the redness of her sores that bothered her now. Redness could be from anything—a mosquito bite from bicycling through the twilight, an allergic reaction to a shrimp cocktail. It was their *crust*, these obscene mesas of dead, dry skin that made her arms look like they were growing scales. A bastardization of the kind of silky skin a pageant queen—an all-American girl—was supposed to have.

Redness could be covered, disguised, neutralized. But crust could not.

Maybe she could rip the scabs off. The skin was dead, after all. It shouldn't hurt. There was no need for the blunt edge of a nail; all she had to do was grab and pull. She could keep her promise to Irene and keep her gloves on—not that it mattered much. And who knows, under the thickest slabs of magma-like crust, maybe her skin would be new and healed and baby-smooth. Maybe this skin disease was actually a revolutionary exfoliation ritual. Maybe it would all be worth it, in the end. She took a deep breath.

She was wrong. It hurt. The scabs stretched instead of breaking. *But we're part of you!* they seemed to sing, clinging to her arm under duress until her vision went white with pain. Ultimately, the determination that Lucrece said was her strongest quality won out. The scabs fought hard, but she tore harder.

Unfortunately, the skin beneath wasn't healed. The sores were still there, looking like perfect circles of refrigerated cherry jam. But at least now they were flat. At least now she could run a butter knife down her arm and not feel a bump.

If she'd been friends with the goth girls at Wanahoo High, they probably would have told her to burn the scabs in a banishing spell. But she hadn't been friends with them—she hadn't really been friends with anyone—and she was afraid to inhale whatever fumes the scabs might release. So she took them out to the yard, to the weeds that had taken over Irene's long-lost flowerbed, and buried them instead.

"And stay there," she said, trying not to feel strangely sad.

A gaggle of girls were gathered around Addison in the Miss Summerall dressing room, breathlessly congratulating her on—what? Her new glamour headshots? The five thousand dollars and rhinestone cowboy hat that she got for winning Miss Pioneer Spirit? Oh, something about a new brand ambassadorship. Another jewelry company? A hair product MLM? No, Angel Dancewear. They made . . . leotards? Veronica wouldn't know. Veronica couldn't dance.

When Veronica first started competing in pageants, she had wanted her talent to be dance. She envisioned herself doing the Charleston in a black flapper dress like a young Ginger Rogers, or pirouetting in a white tulle crinoline like Cyd Charisse. But her body would not cooperate. It could stand up straight and it could hold a pose, but it absolutely could not, would not flow. Every movement staggered and stuttered, as if she was more metal than flesh.

Like so many other graces that had fallen from Heaven since they first started competing against each other as teens, it was Addison who turned into the dancer. Addison's repertoire seemed to consist mostly of jumping and rolling across the floor, kicking her legs, arching her back while pointing her toes—her routines reminded Veronica, cruelly, of a show dog's tricks. But Addison was the one getting leotards for free.

Addison. Addison, who had forced her to wear a wig to school because they couldn't get the headband off at Junior Miss Bliss without shearing a two-inch-wide strip of hair from all around her head. She used to torture herself with questions of what she could have possibly done to deserve such cruelty, before Lucrece told her that if you spent enough time in the pageant world, you could trick yourself into thinking that the people on stage were just dolls.

"Um, excuse me." Veronica hurried over to a harried-looking volunteer with a clipboard and a bright yellow Miss Summerall shirt. "Is there another dressing room?" She was thinking of her fragile legs in that winter gown, of that slice of skin she had to keep pristine for the judges. She was imagining Addison pouncing on her and spraying her with a new poison courtesy of Dr. Gillies, making her entire body burst into red pustules like a river of cranberries.

The volunteer let out an awkward laugh of horrified disbelief. "No, there's just the one."

"Do you have an extra bathroom or something?"

With that she had broken a cardinal sin of pageantry: don't piss off the volunteers. She knew it because this one folded her arms over her chest and let her voice slip from cheery to nasal. "I'm sorry, what exactly is the issue here?"

"I'd just appreciate my privacy."

"That isn't how it works, princess."

By then the other girls had stopped their chatter, their fawning over Addison. They took a break from their dressing, from their pinning and smearing, to watch Veronica lose her mind. She thought she heard someone whisper Addison's favorite nickname for her: "Dairy Queen." She definitely heard someone—Stephanie?—say "psycho."

"Literally, put me in a closet, I don't care. Just don't. Put me. Here. Not with. Her."

The other girls could not contain themselves. The giggles burst the way girls' giggles always did, with cruelty and disbelief. Veronica tried to steel herself. As Lucrece always said, there was no point concerning herself with the behavior of the other girls. She was not here to make friends. Except then she saw Nayeli, getting her dress sewn on by her cousin in the far corner of the dressing room. Nayeli was looking at her in concern. In silence.

"Seriously?" the volunteer swung her clipboard so recklessly she nearly hit Veronica in the face. "Fine. There's a broom closet right around the corner. If you can fit yourself in there, you're welcome to it."

Veronica gathered up her bags and turned her back on the dressing room, muttering a "thank you" to the volunteer that was lost beneath the chorus of giggles and willing herself not to look at Nayeli. It was a relief to close the door on them, even though the hallway seemed to be swaying, dimming, collapsing on itself.

Twenty paces away, the broom closet that would serve as her private dressing room had barely enough space to stand in and didn't seem to have been dusted in years, but at least she was alone. It smelled like a mixture of bleach and mold, but at least in here she'd be safe.

It was just after she shut herself inside it, before she found the lightbulb pull chain, that she saw the other girls covering their teeth as they whispered sordid stories about the madness of poor Veronica. That she saw Addison laughing, open-mouthed.

Addison won Miss Summerall. Big surprise. *May as well just give her the Miss Heartland crown*, she texted Lucrece from the seclusion of the broom closet. *Well, you certainly won't get it with that attitude*, Lucrece replied.

She wanted to snipe back at her that it wasn't her *attitude* holding her back, it was her fucking diseased skin. Christ, after she struck her second pose during the evening dress presentation, she'd taken a glance down at the slit in her dress and watched a new hole burst in her leg. That calf had been perfectly fine one second and then a red pinprick grew—like a drop of food coloring spreading in water—into a perfectly round, raw, dime-sized sore. By the time she got back to her broom closet, an equally awful twin had sprouted right next to it.

I'm dying, she thought. I'm falling apart.

Nayeli stopped by her closet, holding a small trophy commemorating her second runner-up finish. Veronica looked at it in a hunger that filled her mouth with saliva; she didn't know her scores yet, only that she hadn't made the top ten. Considering there were only twenty-four total contestants, she hadn't done this poorly at a pageant since she was sixteen.

"Why are you wearing that dress, silly?" Nayeli's quivering fingers reached toward one of Veronica's skin-tight sleeves, zeroing in like a heat-seeking missile on a hidden patch of sores—as if she could see them through the velvet. Were they oozing? Did they smell? Veronica sharply batted her hand away. "I mean, you knew there was no way they'd like it, right? Maybe if it was Miss Amish Country or something."

"Just felt like it," she muttered. "Thought it would be unique." She threw a glance she hoped was withering at Nayeli. "Thanks for backing me up earlier, by the way."

"Backing up what? You freaking out and stuffing yourself in a closet for no reason?"

"I have to compete too, you know."

She thought Nayeli was angry—but instead she was giggling in a carefree, careless way that made Veronica feel invisible, that made Veronica question every pageant they'd spent together, every inside joke. Nayeli was going on about the rest of the weekend, her plan to sneak off to see Temo, but Veronica had tuned her out so thoroughly that she didn't see her leave.

Her phone shuddered. She had a brief, horrible fantasy about being disinvited from next week's Miss Wickham pageant on the grounds of decomposing—but no, it was a message from Dr. McIndoe. *Lab results from your old prescriptions came back normal*, he wrote. *Attaching them here so you can read them yourself.* She tried looking through the document he'd sent, but after a minute decided to stop kidding herself. It wasn't Dr. Gillies, nor anything he'd sold her. Nothing his office had prescribed had ever touched her leg, and yet. Look.

The door swung open, lighting up the broom closet in a sea of yellow. Veronica's first instinct, aside from shielding her eyes, was to hide her holey leg from view.

Jesus Christ. Well, Addison, to be specific. She was still holding her bouquet of orange roses, still wearing her peacock tiara. She looked so perfect, so still, so ensconced in shadows that her angelic angles looked even more dramatically statuesque, that Veronica wondered if her sores were now causing her to hallucinate. Maybe Addison was here to kill her. In some ways, that would be a relief. She could be remembered as the victim of a zealot, instead of forgotten as a competitor of no consequence, an anonymous failed pageant girl.

"Sorry," Addison said, "I tried knocking."

"Oh. Well. Congrats on your win," Veronica mumbled. "Well deserved."

"Thanks." Addison's voice was flatter, duller than she'd ever heard it. She found herself thinking back to those extra-strength painkillers in Addison's tote bag. "Um, look, I just wanted to say . . ." Addison sighed, her roses drooping in her arms, "that I hope you get the help you need."

That night Veronica peeled off the navy dress one sleeve at a time, terrified and resentful and . . . strangely excited to see what her sores had done while she wasn't looking. It wasn't that she savored this new daily ritual, exactly, but there was a richness in its horror that was hypnotic, almost intoxicating.

Lucrece said the dress had just functioned as a giant bandage around her body, calling attention to the fact that she was ashamed of something. No one likes an insecure pageant queen, Lucrece said—but whatever happened to disguising one's flaws? Didn't Lucrece also preach the gospel of "control every point you can?"

"A flaw is in the eye of the beholder" was how Lucrece had replied to that. It didn't make much sense to Veronica—the "control every point you can" doctrine required an objective assessment of how you lined up against the judges' criteria. Flaws were flaws. A dress that was half-an-inch too short. Eye shadow that was a touch too sparkly. A belly that stuck out. Teeth that were crooked. There was no precedent, no, but wasn't it safe to assume that most judging panels would subtract points for skin that looked riddled with a flesh-eating disease?

The sores being faded was too much to hope for. All she'd done was dab them with antibiotic ointment this morning and cross her fingers that the sores wouldn't sprout more crusted scabs that she'd have to pull off. And lo and behold, they hadn't!

But they had done something else. They had . . . sunken. Recessed. Cratered into her arm so that she could slide the pad of her finger into their indentations. As if they were committed to joining her, forever. As if to remind her that they had risen from her own swamp of a body, from the earth that was her skin.

3. THE WOMAN THAT WAS

"The first reason that you might have lost your last pageant is that you just don't have 'the look.' What's 'the look'? Well, it's whatever *look* the pageant is looking for."

Veronica was experimenting with ways to "plug" the indented sores in her skin while listening to "Five Reasons You Lost Your Last Pageant" on *Pageant World*. Lucrece had told her that if she wore another long-sleeved dress, she might as well not show up to Miss Wickham—but if she showed up as is, they might not even let her into the convention center.

Her first instinct was to smear them with thick layers of liquid concealer—like filling a pothole with asphalt, she figured—but it never seemed to fill the holes up to the surface. Like her skin kept absorbing the concealer before it could harden. Like the indents were actually getting *deeper* by the moment—was that possible? She sighed, watching the concealer drip from the craters. "No Limits," as the Miss Americana website said. No limits to her body's absurdity.

"The second reason that you might have lost your last pageant is that you're what we call a pageant patty—you're too stiff, too nervous, and the judges think you're a robot."

She tried a bit of adhesive putty that she'd used to put up her posters of Audrey Hepburn and Princess Grace—posters that she should have been putting up on the walls of a dorm room, but *never mind*—but it refused to stick to her skin. It was frustrating, but a little slice of her actually felt weirdly proud. Proud of her skin for so decisively neutralizing the putty. For defying her attempts to bring it to heel.

"The third reason that you might have lost your last pageant is that you used too many clichés in your interview. You weren't creative enough in your answers."

So then she tried toothpaste, which nestled into the gaps without much protest. She covered the minty freshness with foundation and she could pretend, if she squinted, like she was once again the person she used to be. Maybe the solution.

"The fourth reason that you might have lost your last pageant is—well, this is a tough one, maybe the toughest one to fix. But it's possible you aren't surrounded by the right people."

She thought of Nayeli, who'd been distant since Miss Summerall. *Just busy*, Nayeli said. Her best friend. Her only friend.

She pulled up Nayeli's profile and zoomed in on every picture Nayeli had taken with Addison, even the ones that Veronica herself was in. Scrutinized the level of affection in every comment between them, the number of heart and fire emojis. When Nayeli was distracted on her phone, was she really texting Temo? Or was she reporting back on her awkwardness to Addison, so they could share laughs at the expense of Veronica the Dairy Queen?

Or maybe it had nothing to do with Addison at all. Nayeli's posts had always blurred the lines between cryptic and inspirational—Veronica had seen her reading books on the power of attraction—but recently her language had bordered on belligerent. Things like, "don't ever let them see you coming" with a knife emoji. Or "if you want it as bad as you say you do, then you'll let nothing stop you, NOTHING." Maybe Addison wasn't so much a co-conspirator as she was next. The thought of Addison the Perfect covered in dents like a hail-hit car made her snort, until she remembered that for this theory to be true, her every happy memory with Nayeli had to be a lie.

She started looking through Nayeli's hundreds of mutuals, looking for people who might know something about skin diseases. Bioweapons. There was somebody named Dr. Kimura, whose expertise was "natural" medicine. There was somebody named Jason, who worked at a pharmaceutical company. There was a personalized cosmetic start-up called Cleave that could have mixed a poison into a small, easy-to-carry delivery package—lip balm, maybe. Something that could be smeared around the rim of a water bottle. Something that could be loaned to a target with friendly ease.

Veronica forced herself to look away. Had Nayeli ever actually liked her? Or had she just tolerated her desperate overtures for friendship because they were so often stuck next to each other in line, *Muenster* coming right after *Mora* in the alphabet? On her limbs, the toothpaste started to sting.

"The fifth reason that you might have lost your last pageant is that you actually want it too much. Sounds crazy, I know! But when you want something that bad, it can totally warp your perspective. You develop this tunnel vision, where the only thing you can see is the crown, and everything else goes dark."

Veronica sat huddled with her knees up to her chest in a corner of the dressing room provided to the Miss Wickham contestants, trying not to make eye contact with anyone. While the other girls twirled in half-zipped gowns, spinning their hair around their wrists to display their delicate wing-like scapulae, Veronica hid inside her trench coat. Not just for privacy, but for warmth. As her holes had deepened—down to three centimeters, now—her body seemed to have lost some of its ability to retain heat.

When she saw Nayeli with her family, Veronica actually felt her stomach flip. She bent her head, hoping she wouldn't be noticed as they set up Nayeli's battle station. Half an hour later, Nayeli hurried over with an energy drink-fueled smile, motioning for her to take off her headphones—and Veronica sternly shook her head. *What's wrong?* she saw but didn't hear Nayeli say. Veronica averted her eyes, so she wouldn't see Nayeli say anything more.

The pageant staff cleared the dressing room for competitors only, so Lucrece had to go—but thankfully, so did most everyone else. "You're radiant," Lucrece said, smoothing her hair. "Just be confident. The judges will see your beauty, trust me."

She still kept her trench coat on as long as she could, finally wiggling out of it just before she stepped out of the shadows of stage-right. She swore she could feel the toothpaste wiggling in her holes with every rattling step she took. She found herself holding her breath to try to keep it sucked in.

"Here's our first question," the main judge asked her once she reached center stage. "What makes you different from the other girls competing for the Miss Wickham title?"

An easy question, thank God, one that Lucrece drilled her on every time they met. "Well, before I answer that, I just want to say that I think all the girls here are incredible and amazing competitors . . . " But then she trailed off, because Lucrece had also drilled into her head that she had to make frequent gentle eye contact with the judges, and the judges were currently furrowing their eyebrows at her in alarm.

In a moment, she realized what had happened. The stage lights were hot, and the toothpaste was melting. Seeping through the foundation and dribbling down her arms in thick, creamy chunks. It looked like she was leaking vanilla custard.

One of the judges—a beautiful man in his thirties—abruptly gagged into his handkerchief and had to excuse himself, though he only made it a few carpeted yards before he had to lean his head into one of the giant hotel trash cans and unleash a series of loud retches that echoed across the ballroom: women into their tote bags, men into their elbows, children and babies anywhere.

The main judge cleared her throat. "Anyway. Please continue, contestant number five."

The only thing she could think to want was the trench coat she'd left on the floor of stage-right. She felt naked as she stumbled around the back of the stage, moving as quickly as she could with her hands over her sores, but not quickly enough to dodge the whispers of a couple girls she passed along the way: *"Swiss Cheese."*

Veronica stared into the dressing room mirror, summoning the will to use the energy she was saving from sitting down to squeeze new pea-sized dots of toothpaste into the weeping holes of her body. To fix in the span of half an hour what she had spent two hours meticulously crafting this morning.

A sharp gasp rose up from the clothing rack behind her. Nayeli had come back to the dressing room, apparently to get a roll of hem tape. Her cousin did all her tailoring; sometimes her outfits fell apart. "Oh my God," she said, "what happened to your arm?"

"I don't know," Veronica replied, honestly. "What do you think?"

Nayeli didn't answer. She only yelped: "You're bleeding!"

"No." In some ways, that would be simpler. Stigmata. Blood loss. She would faint; without medical intervention she would die. She could stop. This could end. "I'm not."

Nayeli knelt down next to her, clasping her hands in prayer. "Did somebody hurt you?" she whispered, and because she couldn't tear her eyes away from the cluster of cavities in the crook of her left arm, she seemed to be asking them the question.

"I don't know," Veronica said again, because the sores weren't going to speak. "My new doctor says I'm doing it to myself. But you'd think if I was going to pick my skin, I'd choose a spot that wouldn't show all the time. Like my stomach, you know."

"Excuse me, is he high? Why the fuck would you do this shit to yourself?"

It was a relief, she had to be honest, to hear someone else say what she was thinking. "Because I'm under so much stress," she said, sarcastically. "But hey, it means one less competitor for you though, right?"

Nayeli sniffled. "Bitch, shut up. You know I wouldn't want to compete without you."

Nayeli was the first person who wasn't a board-certified dermatologist who she allowed to touch any of her sores. Irene had expressed no desire to; she'd said no to Lucrece. Nayeli touched her gingerly at first, too cautious to really pack the toothpaste in—but within a minute, she toughened up. At one point, she even licked her finger before wiping away an extra bit of paste to level off a hole. It touched Veronica, Nayeli's dedication to her repair.

Veronica could see Nayeli's hand flying up to wipe her heavy lashes—it was as if the girl could feel tears preemptively itching at her ducts—and quickly grabbed her wrist. "Don't touch your eyes," she muttered. "They're perfect."

"Aren't you upset?" Nayeli asked.

She stared into the mirror, into the empty porcelain plate of her face. "Yeah. I guess so." She squinted, giving tears permission to flow if they wanted. They didn't. Her heart was a boulder. No, too organic. Too likely to chip. Her heart was plastic, and would not disintegrate for a hundred years, even though her flesh now found it so easy to falter. "I mean, yes, I am."

Nayeli glanced at the clock; she had to go, she said. "See you out there for talent," she whispered.

But when it came time for Veronica to emerge from the dressing room, she could not make herself go. She couldn't do it to herself—poor melting *Swiss Cheese*—and it hardly seemed fair to subject the judges to another nauseating viewing of her corrupted body, either. She stood, took two practice strides, and felt her eyes crossing, her head lolling. The only thing that made her feel safely tethered to planet Earth was dragging two overloaded clothing racks back to her corner of the dressing room and making herself a little cage. A little protective shell, for her *and* the rest of the world.

After twenty beautiful minutes of reprieve, the door swung open and after a flurry of steel heel taps she'd recognize anywhere, Lucrece pulled apart the dresses serving as her curtains and stuck her head beneath the top bar of the clothing rack. "What are you doing? What's wrong?"

"I'm not going back on stage like this."

"Why not? It's not like it's going to get any worse!"

Was she joking? Could she not see? She could not possibly be paying Lucrece enough to lie to this level. "Because there's no point. Literally! There are not enough points I could win by doing anything else to make up for the fact that I look like a melting candle. I can't *win*."

"Is getting a plastic crown the only thing that matters to you?" Lucrece hissed, baring her teeth. "Because if you really need one, I can buy you one off the internet for ten dollars. I thought you wanted to be a future leader of America, a role model for young women? Not all the little girls who'll be watching you in the audience can win plastic crowns, but they can see you walk out there with courage and pride!"

Burning shame welled inside Veronica's throat. But no courage, and no pride.

"Now come on. I told the judges you were throwing up and they agreed to let you go last. So go get yourself out there." Lucrece pointed to the door, and beyond it the site of her humiliation: the stage. Veronica wondered if she had dripped onto its hardwood floor. If they'd had to clean up before letting the next contestant walk on, put up a sign that said Caution: Slippery When Wet. "Now."

Veronica clenched the chair. "No."

At which point Lucrece stormed off, angrier than Veronica had ever seen her in their five years of working together. The dresses in their plastic veils fell back into place with a soft rustle, and though her heart was aching, Veronica could once again breathe.

Veronica stayed long enough to hear them announce the winner. *"Your new Miss Wickham . . . contestant number eight, Nayeli Mora!"* She smiled at that before slipping out the back door in her carefully-buttoned trench coat, hurrying to get out before anyone saw her precisely coiffed hair and realized that she was out of place, on the run, a coward.

When she got home, Irene was waiting in the dark in her hideous old robe, curled around the hideous old table lamp. "Oh, thank God," she said, when Veronica told her what had happened at Miss Wickham.

Thank God?

"Honey, look at you."

Yes, she had done plenty of that. She had spent all day looking at herself. She'd bet her bottom dollar that in the past month she'd spent more time scrutinizing herself in the mirror than Irene had spent looking at her at all.

"You need to get whatever is going on with your skin under control before you go to any more pageants. I mean, I don't even know what you hope to accomplish at this point."

Irene had no understanding of the grit that had to steel up the spine of a pageant queen. She had been a cheerleader in high school. And not a competitive one. Just a run-of-the-mill pom-pom tosser who got on the team because she was blonde and thin and friends with the right queen bees. She'd never faced the judgment of anyone except the men she'd married.

"I'm just trying to protect you, sweetheart. I know how upset you get when you lose."

"It's not about *losing*," she snapped, a bit too ferociously to make her point. "It's about the fact there's only three preliminaries left and if I don't win one of them, I can't even go to Miss Heartland, let alone get a shot at Miss Americana!"

"There's always next year," Irene mumbled, unfussed by Veronica's fury. She was slumped over toward the lamp now, eyes closed but lips somehow still mumbling. "Miss Americana isn't going away."

But her flesh was, wasn't it? Next year she might be nothing but bone. Next year she might not have enough skin and hair left on her skull to hold a crown.

4. THE WOMAN IN WHITE

Veronica did not turn on the ceiling light on the day of the Miss Maddox pageant, even though there was no daylight at six a.m. in the guest room. She crawled to her clothes by the wobbly light of her phone instead. It was better for her, these days, to get dressed in the dark. She did not want to risk seeing any signs of red blisters creeping up her neck, because she did not know how deep those lesions could drill once they reached the cratering stage.

She had moved to the guest room (small, never used) in an attempt to circumvent a possible infestation in her own bedroom. An infestation of what, she wasn't sure. But the fact that the lesions had continued to deepen even after she tried every DIY hack to healthier skin—stopped every dermatological treatment except soap and water, paused the juice cleanse and switched to a diet of omega-3 and vitamin C, bought an air purifier—had made her think about rodents nibbling her sores at night. Invisible insects rooting in the holes.

It was during this self-imposed quarantine that the sores had finally eaten all the way through her limbs. The first time she managed to stick her fingers through her arm, bringing her thumb and middle finger to meet inside what should have been solid flesh as if to turn herself into a human daisy chain, she went woozy and passed out. It took her another month to be able to look at herself in a mirror without needing to lie down and close her eyes and pretend to be someone else.

By the time she came to her senses—by the time she remembered herself—Miss Maddox was the only local preliminary left. She'd begged Lucrece to help her prepare for it. No, not prepare: there was no time to simply prepare. There was only winning, now, and losing. There was no other way to Miss Americana. *Only if you promise to be fearless*, Lucrece said, *and to wear your skin with pride.*

What this meant, in practice, was no more long-sleeved dresses. No bandages, no clay. Veronica had considered learning how to graft skin from hidden parts of her body onto her holes—she might come out looking like a rag doll, but surely that was better than looking moth-eaten—but Lucrece's ultimatum took that option out, too. That was probably for the best. Veronica did not trust her ability to thread a needle now, let alone perform field surgery.

She slowly dragged herself and her bags down the stairs, where Irene ambushed her. It was strange, to see Irene dressed so early. "I talked to the doctor," Irene said. "He says you need to go to the hospital right away. So let's go."

There was this girl, Kayla, who she and Nayeli used to drink sugary juice boxes with on the carpets of shitty hotels across the region. Kayla's mother took her out of pageants when she was thirteen because, apparently, Kayla was very sick. Kayla had postural orthostatic tachycardia syndrome. Kayla had chronic fatigue syndrome. Kayla had chronic Lyme. Kayla had to travel to see a specialist. Kayla needed surgery to get a port installed in her body. On the pageant circuit, everyone was sure of the real reason for all of Kayla's illnesses: Kayla's mother didn't want her to compete in pageants anymore.

Sometimes she and Nayeli would distract themselves from their nerves while waiting for results to be announced by drinking energy drinks and speculating: what had happened to Kayla? Was her mother keeping her bedridden? Had her mother put her in hospice? Was she dead?

Kayla had been thirteen. And Veronica was twenty-one. "I'm not going to the hospital," she said, tugging the bags down the last step of the staircase. "I have the pageant today."

"You have holes in your body, Ronnie, they could be infected."

Ronnie. Her baby name. Was she a baby now? A baby for her mother to mind?

"I'm going to the pageant. Lucrece is picking me up."

"No. Veronica. Stop. I know you don't look in the mirror anymore, but you look worse than ever. As your mother, I'm telling you to stop."

The only thing she needed to stop, Veronica thought, was letting fear rule her heart.

She tried pushing past Irene. Irene tried stopping her. She tried to resist. And Irene's thumb slipped into a hole on her right arm. The sensation plucked some string inside her that made her nearly faint while Irene recoiled, her face twisted into an expression Veronica couldn't read. Was it disgust? Amazement? And then a determination that she had never before seen on her mother's face overcame that expression, and Irene grabbed her by those very holes. As if she was prepared to pull Veronica's arms off, to make her stay.

And maybe Irene would have finally won a fight against her—had Lucrece not started banging on the door. The top of her head was bobbing in and out of visibility through the transom window above the door—she must have been jumping. "Hello!" she was yelling. "Veronica, we have to get going! Hello!"

"Fucking Christ," Irene muttered, squinting as Lucrece's banging got to the headache that always seemed to be lurking just beneath her skull. She left Veronica on the floor while she marched to the door and opened it. Not wide enough for even Lucrece to slip her way in; just wide enough for Veronica to see a sliver of her savior. "Sorry you had to come all this way, but she isn't going to be taking part in any more competitions."

"I know you've been worried about Veronica," Lucrece said, "and I've been worried too. But she's got her pep back now. Let's support her, shall we?"

"What do you mean, got her pep back?" Irene pulled the door open another few inches, enough to display Veronica struggling to sit up on the floor. "She's sick, extremely *sick*, look at what she's done to herself! You can literally stick a fork *through* her!"

Shame. Horror, even. But mostly shame at a body that was being consumed by an invisible mouth, a body that was not so much a body as a condemned house, a moth-eaten dress. She glanced up at the woman who'd been her gut-check for the past five years, and when Lucrece smiled at her without flinching, Veronica could have cried. "She wants to compete, let her compete," Lucrece said. "She's a grown woman."

"No, she's not, she's a child!" Legal age. Twenty-one. "And she is mentally ill—oh!"

Lucrece had shoved her shoulder against the door and scraped her way into the house. When she descended upon Veronica, gently asking her if she could stand, all Veronica really wanted to do was collapse against her. But Lucrece had been right, when she was banging on the door earlier—they had to get going. They got her up awkwardly, Veronica panting with effort and digging her nails into Lucrece's leather jacket. Lucrece's designer sunglasses tumbled off her head with a clatter—"leave it," she said, "it's nothing."

Yes, all this was nothing. The stage was everything. Lucrece grabbed the garment bag with one hand as the two of them struggled out the door with all the grace of a pair of contestants in a three-legged race, Lucrece calling back at Irene to "bring out her makeup bag, please?"

Yet when Veronica twisted her neck around, Irene was just scowling on the welcome mat, her arms folded tightly as if to keep them from accidentally doing something useful.

She decided to appeal to Irene's newfound maternal instinct. *"Mom!"*

Nothing changed on Irene's face. But she did grab the cosmetic case and drop it on the stoop with a disturbing rattle before slamming the door. Hopefully Irene hadn't broken a mirror.

Veronica slipped into the backseat of Lucrece's car—their getaway car—while Lucrece went back to collect the cosmetic case. She crawled in, slithered across the leather, put her head down. There was no sense exerting herself by trying to sit up on the drive to Maddox. She needed to save her strength for the competition.

A tornado had blown through Maddox several weeks before the pageant. FEMA trailers were set up on the outskirts of town for families whose houses had been flattened; some residential blocks looked like they'd been spat out of a giant woodchipper. The town council had considered canceling the pageant altogether, but ultimately decided that maintaining this tradition would symbolize the town's defiance in the face of destruction. "Maddox Strong," the banner above Main Street read.

The truth was that Miss Maddox had never been a premier preliminary for Miss Americana, landing at the end of the local competition season as it did. It was for the dregs, the stragglers, the girls who hadn't already secured their place in the regional competition; the last refuge of the crown-chasers who didn't know when the world was telling them no. No Miss Maddox had ever won Miss Heartland Americana, "but there's no reason why you can't be the first," as Lucrece said.

The convention hall had been destroyed, so they were holding the competition on a baseball field, with contestants prepping in locker rooms and under the bleachers, prancing toe-first to keep their heels from getting stuck in the soil. Preteen boys leaned over the fence across the road, gawking and laughing and making jerking-off gestures. Normally at least a couple girls from Maddox proper would be taking part—a fun little "why not" before finishing up the school year—but this year, those girls were needed at home.

All that meant there were only six contestants in Miss Maddox. Only five girls to beat. One of whom was staring at Veronica while her mother sprayed her hair with something that could punch a hole in the ozone. "What is up with that girl's skin?" her little competitor said. Her mother glanced Veronica's way, squinting as she sized her up. "Don't stare," she told her daughter, who kept on staring nonetheless, "she probably got hurt in the tornado."

Lucrece came to her little corner of the bleachers after scouting the competition and said, "They're nothing. They're just . . . livestock. Crispy hair, glitter shadow. Easy peasy, for you."

But nothing felt easy to Veronica, anymore. "You can see through my body," she said, and Lucrece hurried to stoop to her as if in prayer—in prayer to Veronica in her satin white dress that pooled around her folded legs as if to trap her in a frozen pond.

"Yes," Lucrece said, nodding with excitement. "That's the beauty, don't you see?"

Miss Maddox was late kicking off. They had issues setting up the stage. Rehearsal took a while, because several of the girls had never competed in an official Miss Americana preliminary before. One judge was a no-show until two hours past the designated start time, when he turned up drunk. So it was night by the time the talent portion started. Veronica was second to last in the line-up, and one of the judges seemed to be asleep when she tottered up on stage.

"Hello," she said. "My name's Veronica Muenster, and I'm going to be singing 'His Eye Is on the Sparrow'."

The drunk judge leaned forward. "Go ahead, sweetheart. Please."

"Why should I feel discouraged?" She could feel the stadium lights shining through her body, warm and buoyant and comforting. Until she saw the gold flooding from her body, she had not realized how flat and dull she'd been before the holes. How much she, and everyone else, had simply swallowed light. "Why should the shadows come?"

She heard one of the judges—the one who'd fallen asleep—mumble, "Oh God," as if they were afraid. And they would be right to be. Because Veronica was not a sparrow transformed into a swan. She was a black hole transformed into a star.

"Why should my heart be lonely, and long for heaven and home?"

The night was quiet, so quiet that she could hear the thinness of her voice. She did not have a voice for radio; she was not cut out to be a singer. She was cut out to be an idol. Stolen, smashed, worshipped.

"I sing because I'm happy, I sing because I'm free, for his eye is on the sparrow, and I know he watches me."

She exhaled away from the microphone, waiting. At first all she heard was the violent thudding of her heart, thrashing like a worm on a summer sidewalk against her ribs.

But then the drunk judge stood up, pushing his folding chair over into the dirt, and started to applaud.

Nayeli called that night. A video call that Veronica was glad to be able to answer in pitch darkness since Irene had apparently gone to bed early. "Congrats, Miss Maddox," she said. "Thank God you'll be at regionals. I would have killed myself if I couldn't bitch to anyone."

"Thanks. Are they calling me Miss Paddocks yet?"

Nayeli's lip dropped dramatically in one corner. "Um . . . "

"So, yes."

"You know what, don't worry about it. There's been a lot of weird comments."

A knot pulled tight in Veronica's stomach, even though she wasn't surprised, exactly. She did, after all, look weird. No, not weird—*remarkable,* Lucrece would call it. One of the mindset hacks that Tanya O'Dell had mentioned on that one episode of *Pageant World* was "use nice words to describe yourself: you're not short, you're petite; you're not snippy, you're sassy." *I'm not weird, I'm remarkable. I'm not covered in holes, I'm adorned with them.*

"Anyway, the reason I called you—other than to say congratulations, of course—is that I think I found something. I've been watching these trypophobia videos . . . "

"What videos?"

"Oh, it's like. Fear of clustered holes. Lotus seedheads. Yeast holes. There's these toads that, like, carry their eggs on their backs so when they hatch it looks like all these little holes on their bodies bursting open and . . . " A full-body shudder moved through Nayeli, whipping her spine like a towel. "I'm actually pretty sure that I have it, this trypophobia thing."

Because you saw me? Veronica wondered. *Because you touched me?*

"It's not an actual condition, dumbass," the surly voice belonged to Temo, who was hovering somewhere just beyond the frame of Nayeli's camera. She was in her bedroom, so he must have snuck in. "It's just people being freaks on the internet, trying to gross each other out. Pretending to be grossed out for clout. Just like you're doing right now."

Gross. The word hung in the air like the stench of spoiled food. *So gross.*

"It is absolutely real, because I absolutely have it," Nayeli snapped back. "You saw me almost throw up last night looking at the cow gut picture."

"Yeah, cuz it's cow guts! It's the same way you get grossed out when you see a smashed up squirrel on the highway. Or a dog that's got the mange. You're reacting the way your brain has trained you to react to a sign of disease. Like oh, fuck, get away from me!"

Nayeli rolled her eyes. "That is not it at all. It's got something to do with high-contrast spatial frequencies that some people are just extra sensitive to."

"It's perfectly normal. You're not special."

"Then why won't you look at these pictures, if being scared of them is so *normal*?"

"Because you aren't actually scared of them, you're *obsessed* with them."

Nayeli turned her attention back to the phone. "This boy, I swear to God. Anyway. I was watching this one video compilation of clustered holes in nature and I saw this one plant that . . . well, look at the picture I sent you."

Veronica opened the message that had just come in from Nayeli. The long leaves of a plant marked with perfectly round holes, as if someone had gone at it with a paper punch. Staring through the empty spaces where leaf matter should be, Veronica's stomach did a somersault—and all of her own clustered holes began to tingle at once.

"Doesn't that look like what's going on with you?"

"What is that? What's wrong with it?"

"Hang on, I saved it. Okay, it's called shot hole disease. *Coryneum blight.* It's a fungus, I guess, that attacks . . . stone fruit trees? Like cherries and peaches and shit like that."

"Shot hole." For some reason she thought of golf courses, the kind owned by men that sponsored beauty pageants and owned cherry orchards. "Is that like shit hole?"

"No, it's shot hole like a BB gun shot." Nayeli cocked her fingers for emphasis. "God, of course you've never fired one of those."

"Wait, so it infects the tree and leaves these holes in it?"

"Yeah, it says it starts off with . . . lesions and then they dry up and fall away and leave these round . . . holes. 'The holes can appear anywhere on the plant but are most prominent on the leaves'." Nayeli looked nervous, as if she was afraid of causing offense, but Veronica was thinking about herself as a plant, how her arms would be her leaves, reaching for the world. "Do you think you might have . . . touched a tree that had this, or something? Or breathed around it? I'm pretty sure you can get fungal infections by inhaling them."

Off-screen, Temo objected. "Dude, diseases don't jump from plants to people like that."

"Oh, look who's suddenly Mr. Botany over there."

Never mind about any of that, Veronica thought. That was a question she'd have all the time in the world to answer, after she cleaned up the damage that this disease had wrought on her heretofore carefully-preserved body and won all that she could win. "How do you get rid of it?"

"It just says . . . " Nayeli sighed. She had to wet her lips a couple times before finishing her sentence. "To cut off the parts of the plant that are diseased."

"Oh." She imagined throwing her arm down in front of a buzz saw, pulling a tourniquet tight with her teeth. Much like firing a BB gun and riding an ATV, woodworking was not a world she was familiar with. "What happens if you don't? If you just leave it alone?"

It took Nayeli a minute to answer. She could see Nayeli's scrolling phone screen reflected in her glasses and knew if it was taking her this long to speak, she wasn't finding anything good. Finally, Nayeli shook her head and whispered, "I think it just spreads."

So there was nothing else to do but figure out how she'd gotten sick. She'd been sick for so long, by then, that it was not so difficult to imagine the possibility that her wounds would never heal. Occasionally her thoughts hovered on the precipice of a more frightening truth—that the holes would grow and multiply until her body simply disappeared—but she couldn't stay on that cliffside for very long. She would lose her will to search for her killer, if she did. If only those girls who'd called her Swiss cheese could see her now that she'd truly earned the name—now that her limbs were hole-punched, moth-eaten, now that the first of the bulbous red wounds were spreading to her chest.

But they *would* see her again. She had guaranteed it by winning Miss Maddox. They would all see her again at Miss Heartland Americana, unless the holes overtook the flesh first.

She sorted through her closet, holding each item and trusting her body to know when she'd found something important. Mostly, all she felt was a flat sadness, the memory of the healthy body she used to have. When she didn't find anything in her bedroom, she crawled to the bathroom she shared with Irene. And it was there, in the cabinet under the sink, that she found the thing that made her holes throb: a bottle of essential oil. It was for baths, supposedly. She'd used it a couple times, although she couldn't remember exactly where she got it—it looked like one of those home-packaged bottles that witchy women sold at farmer's markets with the claim that the contents had been blessed by the harvest moon or some shit.

What had Nayeli said? *I'm pretty sure you can get fungal infections by inhaling them.*

"Truth & Beauty," the label read, in what looked almost like handwriting. She unscrewed the cap to take a whiff, and as soon as the scent hit her—a slightly musty mix of sandalwood and clary sage—she remembered the difficulty she'd had with the dropper, the relief she felt when even two drops managed to pool out and fill the entire bath.

And she remembered Irene giving her the bottle. Pushing her to "take another one of your steam baths" the week before Miss Pioneer Spirit. Wanting her to "relax," supposedly.

Irene was still groggy from her nighttime sedative when she came slouching down the stairs the next morning. Maybe she'd taken a double dose, because she looked like hell. "Oh," she said when she saw Veronica. "Did you win your pageant?"

"Yes. No thanks to you. Did you know that this thing would kill me?"

Irene paused at the bottom of the stairs. "That's why I tried to take you to the hospital."

"But there's no cure. Right?" She had to keep her heart steady, her hope flattened. Her body wasn't strong enough to endure an emotional crash. "You know there isn't a cure."

Irene squinted at her, blinded by the sunlight streaming into the living room. "Know? What the hell are you talking about, *know*. God knows I'm always the last one to *know* anything about you these days. You're never here. You never talk to me."

The whine in Irene's voice as she lumbered toward the kitchen made Veronica and her holes recoil with disgust. That didn't seem truthful out of Irene, and it certainly wasn't beautiful. "What do we have to talk about? What groceries to buy? The latest weird bullshit you saw online? Or maybe you just want to keep me stuck here in this house with you, so you don't have to look at my life, and the fact that I might someday get the fuck away from here. Maybe you're just jealous of your own daughter."

Irene's chin was wobbling, but her eyes were solid steel beams boring across the room, refusing to let Veronica's gaze go. "I want, so much, to be jealous of you, honey. I really wish I was. But all I feel is sad. No, you know what, it's worse than that. It's pity."

"Oh, here we go. You're sad. You feel sorry. No, you don't get to act sad. You did this."

"No, I . . . wait, do you think this is *my* fault? What, because I'm the one that first signed you up for a pageant? Jesus, Ronnie. You know, maybe you're right. Maybe this is all my fault."

There was a time when Irene had been the one coaching Veronica, quizzing her with sample on-stage interview questions, finding the best ninety seconds of singing to showcase, showing her how to stand, how to smile, how to walk. Irene would stuff her mouth with bobby pins while putting up Veronica's hair; she would give her the starting pitch for her Do-Re-Mis. There was a time when Irene had seemed to relish her role as "pageant Mom."

And then, one weekend, it all fell apart. They were late getting on the road and there was a screw-up with the entry forms and something had gotten left behind—she couldn't even remember what, anymore—and they'd ended up screaming at each other in the dressing room. Irene stormed off, telling Veronica she could finish her own hair, even though she knew, didn't she, that Veronica did not have the hang of up-dos? Veronica spent fifteen minutes in an escalating panic, trying to spear and spray her hair into order, until a kind woman put a gentle hand on her shoulder and told her she'd look better with her hair down. "Crispy buns are overrated," she had said, winking. "My name's Lucrece, by the way."

"You know, the only reason I signed you up for Miss Junior Fucking Pioneer Spirit in the first place was because I wanted you to feel beautiful. Because I was tired of you coming home from school all sad because your friends were going to the mall without you, or some boy made fun of you. Because clearly, you didn't believe me when I told you that all you needed was just confidence. A nice smile. People. Like. Positive. People."

But Veronica had never been interested in winning Miss Congeniality. That was what Irene never understood about her daughter.

"I wanted you to go back to school with your chin held high, that's all. But you never . . . " Irene cocked her head, as if finally guessing the answer to a riddle, "you never even heard that message, did you? All those crowns and sashes and little plastic trophies you've got in your bedroom and you never actually got the message. You still can't even smile right, my God!"

"I'm not talking about any of that . . . fucking ancient history! I'm talking about the bath oil you gave me! Truth & Beauty! The stuff that did this to me!"

For a good few ticks of the family's heirloom clock, Irene furrowed her eyebrows at Veronica. And then, finally, the cobwebs cleared, and she spoke. "Oh, that?" she said. "That wasn't me. Lucrece left that for you."

5. THE WOMAN CLOTHED WITH THE SUN

A small housefly was hitching a ride on the window of the bus. Its fragile legs wobbled as its wings fluttered, hapless, in the wind. Veronica wondered if it was terrified, clinging on for dear life like that. Or was it happy to be flying faster, higher, farther than it ever had before?

Lucrece's office was in a small brick building near the city's oldest mall. As the bus rolled up to the Holmes and 48th street stop—and the fly gamely crawled out of view—Veronica stared at the boarded-up windows of what had once been the mall's largest department store, where she and Lucrece had searched for her first pair of six-inch nude patent heels. After they found them, Lucrece had her do a little runway walk in front of the middle-aged men and children sitting on benches waiting for their women, just to get her used to the feeling of eyes on her. "Be the most exciting thing they'll see today," she said. "Change their view of what beauty is, bend their standard toward you."

How old had she been then? Sixteen?

Inside Suite 180 of 4750 Holmes, she found Lucrece sitting at her desk, staring at a window that opened onto a brick wall. She turned when she heard Veronica slide into the room, leaning against the wall for support, and put on a pensive smile. "Hello, darling. You must be very angry with me."

Anger was an interesting way to describe the feeling in her heart. It felt too small for the damage that had been done to her, and yet too big for the will she carried to resist further harm, to condemn Lucrece, to demand revenge.

"I just want you to fix it," she sighed. "Honestly. I won't tell anybody. I won't report you. I just want you to make it right."

The sadness in Lucrece's eyes scared her more than the holes. Control every point you can, Lucrece always said, to make up for the things you can't possibly change, the things you simply have to bear. "There's no fixing it. The blight in the bath oil creates a . . . permanent alteration to your appearance. But darling, darling—there's nothing to fix! You are more compelling, more attractive now than you've ever been!"

It made Veronica want to laugh. "What the fuck does that say about your coaching, if *this* is me at my best?"

"That I know how much you want it. That I know the fire in your heart. You're such a hard worker, Veronica. I would have considered it a personal failure if I had not given you this ultimate advantage."

"You're insane." Insane. Crazy. What had Addison's friends called her? Psycho. A psycho coach for a psycho contestant. The scream inside made her want to dig her nails into the netting of skin she had left, pull it off like mozzarella. *Swiss Cheese.*

And Lucrece really did laugh. "Maybe, yes. I've been in this business for thirty years. It does drive you batty, watching girls flatten themselves into little cookie cutter shapes with their smiles stapled on and their goo-goo eyes glued open. All so the men who run the show can watch the little parade go by and say, 'ooh, that one. That's the one I want.' And the ridiculous bit is, they're just buying variations of the same model. Like shopping for groceries!"

"So what is this, some kind of fuck-you to society?" It hurt, to think of herself as a walking affront, an insult on legs. "Because I didn't sign up for . . . "

"No, darling, it's a reminder of what beauty actually is. Beauty is truth. It's clarity. Vulnerability. Beauty doesn't block out the light, don't you see? Beauty is the light shining through the human soul. Like it shone through you last night, when you were crowned Miss Maddox." She reached her hand out to stroke Veronica's cheek. "I knew the judges would see it, if you just let them see you for who you really are." Veronica twitched at the suggestion that these holes—this blight, as Lucrece called it—was who she *really was*, and Lucrece jerked back her hand, biting her lip. "If we could all be so lucky, to be accepted in our truth."

"Maybe you should have done this to yourself, if you wanted to be—"

"No. No, no, no. I couldn't have done it. My dear, nobody would have seen me."

Veronica had spent so much of the competition season in a state of resistance—resisting what was happening to her body, resisting others' attempts to explain it, resisting death—that the urge to kick back against Lucrece had been practically instinctive. But now she felt her eyebrows twist in understanding, because Lucrece was right. Lucrece was objectively beautiful, far more so than Veronica would ever be. Her Miss Americana run had catapulted her, for a time, into glossy jewelry ads in rich women's lifestyle magazines. But she was too old, now.

"Here." Lucrece held up her phone to a picture of Veronica, crowned, on that baseball field in Maddox. The lights shone through her as if she was a glass Christmas ornament. "You are viral."

What Veronica heard was: *you are a virus.*

"Look at this girl. Elle. Look how she's made herself over today." Lucrece pulled another picture onto the screen. A girl in her bathroom had used gore makeup to give herself wounds that looked, with the right lighting, exactly like Veronica's. *Miss Americana*, she'd captioned it, complete with a tiara emoji. It had over one hundred thousand likes. "And she's not even the real thing. She's just a cheap imitation on a screen. A flatterer. But you see how they respond."

The fake stoic look on Elle the Influencer's face—like a high school musical star trying to act—only made Veronica angrier. She smacked the phone out of Lucrece's hand and it went tumbling to the floor. Lucrece didn't even look to see where it landed. "Who cares? That's fucking stage makeup. They're probably impressed she can make herself look like a monster."

"Have you even looked at your own socials, Veronica?"

Reluctantly, Veronica pulled out her own phone and took it off "do not disturb." Her follower notifications were the first thing she noticed. There were so many—her follower count must have quadrupled since she last checked it on the drive to Maddox—that she first thought that she'd been hacked. And then she noticed the number of unread messages.

I can't describe it, but I truly have never seen a woman as beautiful as you.

Please never go out in public where small children can see you. You are a disgrace.

God smiles upon you and your beautiful soul <3

BURN YOUR CROWN BITCH

We don't deserve you, queen. Future Miss Americana.

I would kill myself if I looked as awful as you

She read that one aloud to Lucrece. "It says I'm awful," she said, in case Lucrece didn't understand.

But Lucrece seemed neither able nor willing to understand the weight of that word, the way it pummeled everything Veronica had tried to protect about herself. The *at-least-people-think-I'm-pretty,* the *at-least-I-scored-better-than-them.* Instead of collapsing, Lucrece's smile broadened.

"Yes exactly! Awful!" Somehow coming from her smiling Revloned lips—Crushed Rubies, the shade was called—the word didn't feel quite so heavy. "Didn't they teach you what awful means in English class?"

Veronica narrowed her eyes. She shook her head.

"Awe-ful. Inspiring great awe. That's what it means. Deserving great respect. It means you are . . . " Lucrece dropped to her knees, her wince only barely visible even as the sound of bone hitting tile filled the room, "majestic."

The day before Miss Heartland Americana, Lucrece arranged a meeting with Hebe's North American marketing team to discuss the possibility of a brand ambassadorship. They were tucked away from the rest of the pageant, on the second floor of the Continental Hotel in a room filled with artisanal bottled waters, which Lucrece said was a good sign.

"They want to snatch you up," she said. With white shift dresses selling for thousands of dollars in European capitals, Hebe would be a much more prestigious sponsor than Forger Foods. Hardly even comparable to Angel Dancewear. Hebe had all sorts of ideas for groundbreaking photo shoots: threading gold chains through her limbs instead of over them; hanging baubles from the holes in her flesh for Christmas. All under doctor supervision, they assured her. Veronica had never heard the words "open doors" so many times.

But she didn't like the way the brand director was looking at her. With greed. She couldn't pinpoint, exactly, what the greed hungered for—except that it left her feeling sure that he collected trophies. Two-headed calves. Cat mummies. Shrunken heads.

Veronica turned her head toward the window so she wouldn't have to look at him. Peering down at the street, she saw that the religious nutso who'd yelled at Addison to "take off your crown" at Miss Pioneer Spirit was across from the hotel. He'd brought his bullhorn again.

If she was Addison's father's daughter, the Hebe guy wouldn't have dared look at her that way. He would have known that he'd have ended up knocked out cold. But she wasn't Addison's father's daughter, and Irene wasn't here to stick up for her. She was at home, tending to the strange, pale little plants that had grown out of the scabs Veronica had planted. Watering them, sprinkling them with plant food, giving them little umbrellas when she was afraid the sun would be too much for them. Being a good mother.

After the meeting ended, she slipped away from Lucrece and the men from Hebe before he could get close enough to touch her. She rode the escalator down to the lobby to put more distance between them and then kept walking, leaning against planters and columns, imagining getting on the first truck that would let her lay down in its bed before remembering the crown. How badly she wanted the crown.

Could she hire bellhops to protect her? No. What about

security guards? She saw some loitering outside, past the sliding doors. She had to put on her jacket to get the motion sensor to detect her, then stumbled into the heat.

The security guards were laughing at the protesting man across the street. Calling him a loser, a hater, saying he was fucked in the head to hate beauty pageants so much. "Surprised they don't call the cops," one said, even though he wasn't breaking any laws. They were too weak, Veronica decided. Not enough conviction. Not enough passion. Too willing to pass the buck.

But then there was the protesting man. The nutso. "Why dress yourself in scarlet and put on jewels of gold?" he was yelling on the curb of the carwash. "You adorn yourself in vain! Your lovers despise you! They want to kill you!" He might have the strength of character necessary to defend a girl in need.

She teetered across the street, even though Lucrece wouldn't want her to expend any more energy than she absolutely had to, and uncrossed her jacketed arms as she approached the man. He immediately averted his eyes and started yelling words like "begone!" and "devil!", like a priest warding off a vampire.

Unfortunately for him, these words had no impact on her. "Look at me," she said, rolling her shoulder, and then her arm, out of its sleeve. Her muscles were weak. It took a while. After she was done, it took the last reserves of her depleted energy to stand there, swaying like one of those floppy inflatable balloon-people that got staked down at car dealerships, letting the sun and the smoke and all the acrid scents of uncollected garbage seep through the prism of her body.

It started with his silence. Then the silent mouth began to tremble, like he was about to cry, and the silent neck leaned backward while the silent shoulders drooped. It was as if the blight had suddenly released him from all the rules he had spent his life following, all the braces that had held him upright, and now he was custard. He was jelly.

And then she too was released by her body, crumpling like a puppet whose strings had been cut. From a distance it probably looked like she'd fainted, but her eyes were wide open on the sidewalk, staring at the man. He had followed her down, dropping his bullhorn and flattening himself against the hot grainy asphalt so that he need not look down at her, apparently. His chapped lips kept parting, then closing, then parting again—as if he wanted to say something.

"You can speak," she told him, and his jaw dropped open. So she was rebuilding him.

"Angel," he whispered, "You have no flaw."

Veronica smiled. You could take the man out of his church, but you couldn't take the church out of the man.

"Take me back to the hotel," she said.

He immediately leapt up to do so, wrapping her up in her jacket so as not to touch her skin directly. It wasn't disgust, she could see that. It was reverence. Lucrece had told her that the blight had a power that couldn't be predicted, one that might manifest very differently for different audiences—it urged the Hebe brand director to possess, while it called this man to serve. Which was how Veronica learned that beauty was subjective, after all.

On the first day of competition, people thronged around the woman who held light in her body—contestants and their relatives, the army of volunteers and vendors who staffed Miss Heartland Americana, respected members of the pageant's board of directors. It wasn't hate in their eyes, no. They were curious, craning their necks, touching the spots on their own bodies where Veronica's holed body carried light. Not even her competitors could hate the gilded being whose steps they now followed, awe-struck. But there was a pressure in their proximity that put what little skin Veronica had left on high alert. Theirs was a hunger that refused to share.

The protesting man—now no longer protesting—pushed them all back with the zeal of a man who had seen God. He didn't care who he shoved. When a middle-aged volunteer woman ran up to try to get a photo with Veronica, he grabbed her by the collar and threw her like a wrecking ball into a throng of people. Veronica only had a second to glance back at the mass of upturned bodies before Lucrece hurried her down the hallway, because they needed to get to the dressing room by five p.m. Now that Lucrece was solely responsible for makeup and it took Veronica twice as long to get in and out of her clothes, they needed all the time they could get. Having holes where uninterrupted muscle and bone should be had given Veronica a debilitating fear of tearing.

Her fellow Miss Heartland Americana contestants were all in on the latest beauty trend. Who knows how it had started. One girl saw another girl try it, and get a thousand "likes" of validation. One girl clicked on a trending hashtag. One girl heard about it from her coach, or her mother, or her dermatologist. One girl listened to the latest episode of *Pageant World*: "Five Ways to Pull Off This Summer's Boldest Look."

Boldest. Sickest. Most Blighted.

And these girls weren't dotting on red and black eyeliner, they weren't applying paper-mâché prosthetics. They were changing themselves for good, burning and carving clustered holes into their bodies while rehearsing their interview answers: "I always had a voice, but the crown will give me a microphone . . . " "I didn't choose my platform, my platform chose me . . . " "As Miss Heartland Americana, I will . . . "

That was the thing about pageant girls, the one true thing after all other pillars fell into doubt. They always committed, to whatever they did.

Girls were using whatever they could get their hands on—a lot of cigarettes bummed off the security guards, a lot of needles from their sewing kits, but Addison, of course, had access to the best: a hot knife, plugged into the wall in place of her curling iron.

Amid this chaos, Veronica alone was still. Lucrece was vigorously teasing her hair into a bouffant. Every so often Veronica would ask if there were any signs of blight on her head—because surely she would die, wouldn't she, if a BB-sized hole opened up through her skull?—and Lucrece would say, "no, no, no" in a tone that Veronica didn't quite believe. The truth, she supposed, would be revealed soon enough. It was a lot like blight, in that way.

To avoid looking in the mirror for too long—she found it gave her migraines—Veronica scrolled, only semiconsciously, through the notifications on her phone. Most of the posts she was tagged in were pictures of a blonde woman she barely recognized as herself—some of them blurry paparazzi-style shots, some of them watermarked pageant photos. But there were also a few strangers who apparently wanted to feel her gaze through the internet. Strange, for someone to desire *her* to look upon *them*. Among these strangers was a middle-aged woman in a Miss Heartland volunteer shirt, proudly tilting her face to the camera to better display the bruises and scrapes she'd gotten falling through the crowd. *So happy to have met the lovely Veronica,* she'd written. *And look at my gorgeous souvenirs!*

"It's the woman who wanted a picture with me," Veronica said. "She's hurt."

"Aren't we all," Lucrece said, frowning as she gingerly pulled a boar bristle brush over the crown of Veronica's head. "Eat your energy bar. It's fifty grams of protein."

Somewhere in the dressing room, Addison was screaming. Veronica would recognize that voice anywhere. That mouth, open and teeming with orthodontically-perfected teeth.

The Venus Ballroom was packed, and vibrating with anticipation. There had to be a thousand hearts pitter-pattering, two thousand lungs hyperventilating in Veronica's direction. A few stray camera flashes went off as Veronica entered stage left, but a soft murmur of the microphone quickly reminded the audience that there was to be no flash photography.

Her blighted legs felt so light that they almost seemed made of cotton candy. Save for brief flashes of electric pain when she had to hoist each heel up and forward, she might have felt like she was gliding. Or sinking. Or falling. Fortunately, Lucrece had sewn ribs of sturdy coat hanger wire into the sides of her dress that were helping her stay upright, so all she had to worry about was pushing her cotton candy legs toward the central X.

She knew when she'd reached it because a thousand throats gasped as the lights lined up behind her blighted body. "My name is Veronica Muenster," she said, leaning ever so slightly toward the mic. "I'm going to be singing 'Abide with Me'."

Such a melancholy song would never scoop up the talent points needed to win Miss Heartland, which was why Lucrece had pushed her to repeat "His Eye Is on the Sparrow." It had been her lucky charm at Maddox, after all. But Veronica had felt strongly that this occasion called for a different vibe. "I don't want to sing about someone else watching over me," she told Lucrece, "while I'm the one watching over them."

Besides, winning was no longer the objective, was it? Winning was superfluous to their mission of the blight. Winning was child's play.

"Where is death's sting? Where, grave, thy victory?"

As soon as she started singing, holes burst in the judges. Only one of them cried out in pain; the others swallowed the force of the injury, out of their deep respect for Veronica the Majestic. Blight burst apart their ear lobes and turned flesh into flags, fluttering on the faint breeze of the air conditioning.

A confetti-sized piece of human meat that had spun off a judge found the air current and floated sleepily toward the stage. Veronica watched as it veered off to the right of her head, rolling her eyes until they hurt so she wouldn't have to turn her head—and saw Nayeli standing in the wings, eyes brimming with love. Her heart twinged a bit when she saw blood dripping from Nayeli's arm—was she digging holes? No. Nayeli would never risk her manicure if she didn't have to. She was using a pair of nail scissors. Boring them into her arm over and over, like a poorly-aimed corkscrew.

"I triumph still," Veronica sang, reaching forward as if to hold the ballroom, this small snow globe of a world, in her tattered arms, "if thou abide with me."

Subscribe to Crystal Lake Publishing's Dark Tide series for updates, specials, behind-the-scenes content, and a special selection of bonus stories - http://eepurl.com/hKVGkr

THE END?

Not if you want to dive into more of the Dark Tide series.

Check out our amazing website and online store
or download our latest catalog here.
https://geni.us/CLPCatalog

We always have great new projects and content on the website to dive into, as well as a newsletter, behind the scenes options, social media platforms, our own dark fiction shared-world series and our very own webstore. Our webstore even has categories specifically for KU books, non-fiction, anthologies, and of course more novels and novellas.

ABOUT THE AUTHORS

Jessica Landry is a Canadian screenwriter, director, and Bram Stoker Award-winning author. Her collection, *The Night Belongs to Us,* was released by Crystal Lake Publishing in March 2023; she also co-edited the Bram Stoker Award-, Shirley Jackson Award-, and British Fantasy Award-nominated anthology *There Is No Death, There Are No Dead*; and has an original story in *Aliens Vs Predator: Ultimate Prey*, released in March 2022. Her original horror feature, *My Only Sunshine*, was accepted into Whistler Film Festival's Screenwriters Lab in 2020 and is in development with Jessica set to direct. She was accepted into the CFC/Netflix Project Development Accelerator with her original horror/comedy series, *Catastrophe Queens*; as well as TIFF's inaugural Series Accelerator and NSI's Series Incubator program with her original limited drama series, *Ghosts of Lakeland*. Jessica has written several MOWs alongside Neshama Entertainment, including *List of a Lifetime,* which was nominated for a Critics' Choice Award for Best Made for Television Movie. She's worked in the development room for the CBC show *Strays*; has written on *Family First*, a sitcom with Eagle Vision; *7th Gen*, a factual series with Eagle Vision and APTN, which she also directed; and is currently adapting the novel *April Raintree* as a limited series, among other projects in various stages of development. Find her online at jesslandry.com.

Sofia Ajram is a multidisciplinary artist based in Montreal. Prior publications include "The Arborglyph" in the anthology *Lost Contact.* Their latest project, *Bury Your Gays: An Anthology of Tragic Queer Horror* (serving as Editor) releases April 2024. When they're not writing, they can be found goldsmithing at Sofia Zakia or moderating the Horror forum on Reddit. Find them on Twitter @sofiaajram.

Nadia Bulkin is the author of the short story collection *She Said Destroy* (Word Horde, 2017). She has been nominated for the Shirley Jackson Award five times. She grew up in Jakarta, Indonesia with her Javanese father and American mother, before relocating to Lincoln, Nebraska. She has two political science degrees and lives in Washington, D.C.

Readers . . .

Thank you for reading *Little Mutilations*. We hope you enjoyed this 7th book in our Dark Tide series.

If you have a moment, please review *Little Mutilations* at the store where you bought it.

Help other readers by telling them why you enjoyed this book. No need to write an in-depth discussion. Even a single sentence will be greatly appreciated. Reviews go a long way to helping a book sell, and is great for an author's career. It'll also help us to continue publishing quality books. You can also share a photo of yourself holding this book with the hashtag #IGotMyCLPBook!

Thank you again for taking the time to journey with Crystal Lake Publishing.

Visit our Linktree page for a list of our social media platforms.
https://linktr.ee/CrystalLakePublishing

Our Mission Statement:

Since its founding in August 2012, Crystal Lake Publishing has quickly become one of the world's leading publishers of Dark Fiction and Horror books in print, eBook, and audio formats.

While we strive to present only the highest quality fiction and entertainment, we also endeavour to support authors along their writing journey. We offer our time and experience in non-fiction projects, as well as author mentoring and services, at competitive prices.

With several Bram Stoker Award wins and many other wins and nominations (including the HWA's Specialty Press Award), Crystal Lake Publishing puts integrity, honor, and respect at the forefront of our publishing operations.

We strive for each book and outreach program we spearhead to not only entertain and touch or comment on issues that affect our readers, but also to strengthen and support the Dark Fiction field and its authors.

Not only do we find and publish authors we believe are destined for greatness, but we strive to work with men and woman who endeavour to be decent human beings who care more for others than themselves, while still being hard working, driven, and passionate artists and storytellers.

Crystal Lake Publishing is and will always be a beacon of what passion and dedication, combined with overwhelming teamwork and respect, can accomplish. We endeavour to know each and every one of our readers, while building personal relationships with our authors, reviewers, bloggers, podcasters, bookstores, and libraries.

We will be as trustworthy, forthright, and transparent as any business can be, while also keeping most of the headaches away from our authors, since it's our job to solve the problems so they can stay in a creative mind. Which of course also means paying our authors.

We do not just publish books, we present to you worlds within your world, doors within your mind, from talented authors who sacrifice so much for a moment of your time.

There are some amazing small presses out there, and through collaboration and open forums we will continue to support other presses in the goal of helping authors and showing the world what quality small presses are capable of accomplishing. No one wins when a small press goes down, so we will always be there to support hardworking, legitimate presses and their authors. We don't see Crystal Lake as the best press out there, but we will always strive to be the best, strive to be the most interactive and grateful, and even blessed press around. No matter what happens over time, we will also take our mission very seriously while appreciating where we are and enjoying the journey.

What do we offer our authors that they can't do for themselves through self-publishing?

We are big supporters of self-publishing (especially hybrid publishing), if done with care, patience, and planning. However, not every author has the time or inclination to do market research, advertise, and set up book launch strategies. Although a lot of authors are successful in doing it all, strong small presses will always be there for the authors who just want to do what they do best: write.

What we offer is experience, industry knowledge, contacts and trust built up over years. And due to our strong brand and trusting fanbase, every Crystal Lake Publishing book comes with weight of respect. In time our fans begin to trust our judgment and will try a new author purely based on our support of said author.

With each launch we strive to fine-tune our approach, learn from our mistakes, and increase our reach. We continue to assure our authors that we're here for them and that we'll carry the weight of the launch and dealing with third parties while they focus on their strengths—be it writing, interviews, blogs, signings, etc.

We also offer several mentoring packages to authors that include knowledge and skills they can use in both traditional and self-publishing endeavours.

We look forward to launching many new careers.

This is what we believe in. What we stand for. This will be our legacy.

Welcome to Crystal Lake Publishing— Tales from the Darkest Depths.